ON THE SCOUT

THE GREEN COUNTRY SERIES #1

CHARLIE AMOS

Publishing Coordinator – Sharon Kizziah-Holmes
Cover Design – Jaycee DeLorenzo

Paperback-Press
an imprint of A & S Publishing
Paperback Press, LLC
Springfield, Missouri

ISBN: 978-1-964559-55-1 (Paperback)
ISBN: 978-1-964559-56-8 (Hardback)
ISBN: 978-1-964559-57-5 (eBook)

DEDICATION

For Doc and Mary

ACKNOWLEDGMENTS

This book and the others that follow in this series is only possible because of the support and guidance of many people. This story took root many years ago and sat as a dormant seed until I finally took time to strike fingers to keyboard. When I wrote the first draft it was my wife who allowed me the distance and understanding to let me work. Cows, kids, and a full-time job does not allow for much time to write.

When a normal person would turn on a streaming service and relax, I would turn on a word document and try to fill blank pages. It was those times when my wife would let me type or study maps and obscure books. Allowing me to ignore the present and write.

Members who I met at the Western Writers of America conference gave me the confidence to draft a novel. The WWA and its members welcomed me into their community and have taken time to answer questions on the craft and share western history. If not for that organization, I would not be writing this now.

Of course there is you the reader. I wrote this for you. To entertain and hopefully provide a glimpse of history in the development of the western United States. Our history is complex. Our ancestors are legends.

Finally, I would like to acknowledge the Devine providence that placed me here at this time. Who provided the path that I chose giving me the experiences needed to give you this story.

CHAPTER 1

――――◆«◆»◆――――

Turon Turtle rode down the slope and reined a leggy bay to a stop. Dropping the reins he swung one leg in front of the saddle horn and retrieved a tobacco pouch from his pocket.

From the shade of a cottonwood tree Levi Kuratowski looked up from his book and nodded. The Jewish immigrant felt a kinship to the Cherokee cowboy since coming to work on the prairies. Tied to a low limb Levi's roan horse grazed.

Turon carefully rolled a cigarette and dampened the paper with his tongue. Once he had the cigarette built, he balanced it between his lips and offered the pouch to Levi who politely declined. Striking a match on the heel of his boot he lit the cigarette then ensured the match was completely out, as was the custom of people who lived on the grassy plains.

"Still reading that book about shooting the moon?"

"Yes, it's getting good. They are making a shell that these fellows can ride in."

"Ride in? Like a wagon?" asked Turon as he blew smoke from his nostrils.

Levi thought about that before he answered. "More like a barrel."

"Who dreamed up this story?" Turon asked.

"Jules Verne." Levi closed the book.

"What kind of woman has time to write a book like that?" Turon grinned.

"A smart woman. I think it's possible to go to the moon," said Levi. "She describes how we could do it."

"Why go to the moon?" Turon removed a flake of tobacco off his tongue.

Levi stood and stuffed the book into a sack hanging on his saddle.

"Because we could, and no one else has been there." Levi turned to face Turon.

"The Cherokee went there once on a hunting trip looking for deer. There is no grass. So, no need for us to go." Turon took a puff on his cigarette.

"Grass? What does grass have to do with it?" Levi's brow raised.

"No grass. No cows. So, no need for cowboys up there." A wide grin filled Turon's face. "Too far from the market if it had grass," he added.

"I am not going to be a cowboy forever. I am going to buy a wagon and sell goods. Maybe open a store one day," Levi said defiantly.

"Not on the moon." Turon grinned. "Who you going to sell to?"

"Well, I may not go to the moon, but one day people will."

"When they do, they will find the Cherokee have already been there and no deer." Smoke poured out from Turon's nostrils. "Anyway, you ought not read books written by crazy women. You should be keeping these cattle from drifting over to the Osage," Turon scolded.

Levi was ignoring him and watching a rider approach from the north.

Turon turned in the saddle to look in the direction

of Levi's gaze. "Looks like Frank Harper." He swung his legs back into the stirrups.

The black mare Frank Harper rode jumped sideways as a covey of quail launched into flight from a stand of bluestem. A natural rider, Frank never touched hand to saddle as he corrected the mare and scolded her for her flightiness.

As Frank rode closer Levi tightened his cinch and pulled the slipknot tethered to the limb. Frank nodded to them both and stepped down from the black mare.

"Afternoon, gents," Frank said as he moved around to the hindquarters of the black mare. Keeping the horse between him and the others Frank relieved himself soaking the parched earth.

"Mr. Hatcher told me to ride out and bring everyone to the big house." Frank toed some dust over the wet spot on the ground.

"He going to give us a raise?" Turon asked.

"Is something wrong?" Levi rubbed the back of his neck out of habit.

"I don't rightly know what he wants. All I know is a rider came in from Pond Creek three days ago. Mr. Hatcher took the buggy into Caldwell, and he came back late last night. This morning, he said to ride out and bring everyone to the big house."

What the cowboys called the big house was no more than a shack but compared to the dugouts the line riders stayed in it was impressive with a wood range. Wes Hatcher, owner of the Hatcher Cattle Company, had the house built in hopes of keeping his wife nearby. After the first winter in the Cherokee Outlet however, she opted to stay in Texas and oversee their property there.

"Who else you need to gather?" Turon asked.

"You all are the last ones. Everyone else is already riding in. Chubb caught several birds in his quail trap.

He's going to roast them for supper."

"Bad news or good news, we will eat good." Turon grinned.

"Ya, I wonder what news Mr. Hatcher could have." Levi nodded, still appearing anxious and serious.

"You'll have to ask him. He didn't say anything other than to fetch everyone." Frank sounded irritated that he had to repeat himself.

Levi swung into the saddle as Frank tugged on his horse's cinch. Turon and Levi waited on the older cowhand to mount the black mare. Frank jerked the horse's head from the bluestem she was greedily consuming, stepped into the saddle, and led off in the direction of the big house. The three rode out into a sea of grass.

CHAPTER 2

—◆«◆»◆—

Leaning forward in the saddle Wes Hatcher squinted at the three riders approaching the headquarters. He had ridden out earlier in the day to keep his distance from the crew. It had not been an easy decision for him to make. Now as he looked down at the men, he felt the dread of delivering the news.

The cattle venture in the Cherokee Outlet had been a gamble. He borrowed all he could against his ranch near San Saba, Texas. He bought his way into the Cherokee Strip Livestock Association. After selecting his allotment, he drove yearlings from San Saba north to his Cherokee lease. His Texas cattle gained on the tall grass along the Salt Fork and the Arkansas rivers.

After the first year he drove the steers to market in Kansas and kept his heifers that were by this time heavy with calf. Paying off his loan he expanded. This time he spent six weeks in the Cherokee and Muscogee nations buying yearlings in twos and threes until he had gathered enough to drive to his Cherokee lease for fattening on a never-ending supply of grass.

"It's all over now." Wes Hatcher sighed.

The sorrel gelding stood indifferent to the comment and the weight of the rider.

Wes continued talking to his horse. "The federals will open this country up to homesteaders soon. The association won't admit it but that's what will happen."

The sorrel gelding offered no sympathy and stood silent.

"The flats will be plowed under, and the hills grubbed off to the rocks in less than ten years. After that, the grass'll be gone, and the cedars will take over wherever a bird sits on a farmer's fence."

The sorrel continued his indifference.

"Well, might as well get on with it." Wes reined the horse toward the gathering cowboys and gently applied heel pressure to the sorrel's sides.

Riding into headquarters Turon, Levi, and Frank reined up next to the round pen. Ounce Pathkiller, a Cherokee cowboy, was saddling a stout four-year-old pinto that Hatcher traded for across the river in the Osage Nation. The pinto was the last horse Ounce had left to break.

Mr. Hatcher in general was a good judge of horses but a better judge of seeking a profit. Of the twelve horses he got on the trade the pinto was the ugliest. His color pattern made an already large head look huge and his hoofs resembled blackjack stumps. He would make his money on the eleven and the pinto would eventually grow into his head and feet, making a good horse to drag calves to the branding fire.

John Stanley stood by the pinto's head whispering to him in a calming sing-song voice. Next to Ounce, John Stanley was the best horseman in Hatcher's outfit. He had been the youngest of a sharecropper's family in the Muscogee Nation. His parents once belonged to the same Muscogee family they now farmed on shares. John Stanley had jumped on the chance to go with Mr. Hatcher on a cattle-gathering trip through the nations. As he preferred the unknown of a cattle outfit to the familiarity of cotton rows.

Leaning against the rails of the round pen John and Jim Boiling watched the pinto in anticipation of a show. The two brothers looked like copies of one another. Both wore a knowing grin but if one looked at their eyes they conveyed a general confusion.

Their look of bewilderment could have been the result of the last man on the crew. Known as Preacher Bob or simply "Preach" he never let an opportunity to spread the Gospel Word pass. Once a conversation turned idle, he found parallels and a way to turn it toward Scripture.

John and Jim politely followed Preach's impromptu sermon. A sermon that did not yield as Frank, Turon, and the Jewish Levi reined up their horses.

Ounce pulled the cinch tight on the pinto and John Stanley softly explained to the horse what was about to happen.

"Jesus was of the land of Palestine. His message however has gone beyond those holy borders," Preach said trying to hold the Boiling brothers' attention.

The brothers glanced and nodded at the riders in unison ignoring Preacher Bob.

Frank was the last to swing down from the saddle and began letting out his cinch.

"Palestine?" Frank said in a voice to match Preacher Bob's. "I should have known Jesus was from Texas." Frank laughed.

Laughter spread to the brothers who always looked to Frank for guidance and acceptance.

"Blasphemous behavior, Frank Harper. You will burn in Hell for your remarks and sinful ways." Preacher Bob pointed an accusingly boney finger toward the grinning cowboy.

"You better watch yourself, you Bible thumper,

before condemning me to the fiery furnace. You will wish for the Second Coming by the time I am through with you."

The tense situation was abruptly over as John Stanley whooped. Ounce sat in the saddle as the long head of the pinto tucked completely underneath his body. The hoofs struck the ground jarring the Cherokee cowboy whose body absorbed the punishing jumps. As the pinto bucked around the pen Ounce got in rhythm with the horse's lunges. Dust took to the air and the cowboys gathered around the pen's rails yelling encouragements. Ounce blended his movements and matched the pinto's hops and twists. As quick as the horse had begun to buck, he soon accepted the weight of the rider. Ounce began to lope him around the pen then brought him to a stop.

The pinto stood still as Ounce stepped down from saddle. John Stanley caught his head and gave him praises by rubbing the horse's neck.

"Loosened my teeth some." Ounce grinned broadly. "He'll make a stout cow pony."

The cowboys had not noticed Wes Hatcher ride up, sitting on his big sorrel gelding.

Ounce and John Stanley were the first to see the old rancher. Although his hair had gray streaks his eyes still shone with fire and determination.

Wes Hatcher did not speak for a few moments as the men were waiting on him. Chubb, a man old as Wes walked over from the house, a flour sack made into an apron tied around his waist. Flour and dough clung to the hairs around his thick wrists.

"Well, reckon I should get to it," Wes said as everyone waited and listened.

"As you know, the association has filed for an extension with the Cherokees and the Department of the Interior to renew the lease. As it stands, the President of the United States has made it clear that he intends to order all cattle off the Outlet. Might be June of next year or I have even heard that it could come as soon as October first."

The cowboys had heard talk from other outfits of the ongoing negotiations between the members of the Cherokee Strip Livestock Association, the Cherokee Nation, and the federal government.

The land they leased and occupied was technically Cherokee land, provided the federal government did not find another use for it. After the Cherokee Nation took up arms against the United States during the Civil War the Cherokee lands in the west were subject to federal seizure.

"Here's the plain truth of the matter," Wes continued. "In Eighty-five, just four years ago, stockmen on the Cheyenne and Arapaho reservations were given the same directive. Some of you remember what happened that year to those stockmen. Forced to sell their cattle, the markets were flooded. Soon the price of beef crashed."

Frank nodded. He had been one of those cowboys who lost his job when that happened.

"Boys, I am not going to give these cattle away. It is the consensus among the other owners that they are going to hang on and hope the attorneys get this settled." Wes rocked forward, his hands on the saddle horn. "I am selling now while I have a chance to do so. I must think about my place in San Saba. I cannot afford to lose everything here. I have a buyer lined up and he'll take delivery of all cattle in Caldwell."

The cowboys were silent. They all waited to hear more.

"This land was never ours. In eighty-five the president ordered all the structures and pens removed.

I have sold the house for lumber and a carpenter from Caldwell will be out this week to take it down."

"When is the delivery date, Mr. Hatcher?" Frank asked.

"Ten days from now." Wes's face was blank. "I know it's short notice, but we are in a business that can be frozen out by one storm, drowned out in one flood, or written off by one bureaucrat. I will pay you off in Caldwell. You will be paid out this month plus I will let you have your choice of horse from your string. If you don't want a horse, I'll pay you an extra forty dollars. That should leave you plenty for a train ticket and traveling money."

Wes looked around at the cowboys. He was relieved to have that much said and out of the way. "Rest up. Chubb will have dinner ready after a while. Tomorrow, gather your belongings. Cave in your dugouts. We'll start gathering cattle the next day."

Before turning his sorrel toward the house Wes looked at the black cowboy still patting the pinto's neck. "John Stanley, could I have a word with you over at the house?"

"Yes sir." John Stanley climbed over the pen rails in a fluid motion that took little effort. The two went to the house. The older rancher rode while the younger cowboy trotted behind catching up so he could take the reins as Wes climbed down.

Frank was the first of the remaining cowboys to break the silence.

"Well, shit." He looked around at the other men.

"We better give these horses a rub down and let them chase some grass," Turon said.

Levi reached and took Frank's horse.

"Thanks, Little Kansas." Frank turned to walk away.

Several of the men called Levi "Little Kansas." Since he joined the outfit, he had made it known about his desires to open a store in Kansas City. A town he saw as prosperous in much the same way that his relatives had seen New York City in an earlier generation.

As Frank walked away the Boiling brothers followed closely behind.

CHAPTER 3

———◆«◆»◆———

Turon and Levi finished rubbing and combing the horses about the time John Stanley came back from the house.

"Turon," John Stanley said in his thick slow accent. "Mister Hatcher wants a word with you and Little Kansas." Reaching for the lead rope he continued, "I can take the horses down to the creek bottom. There's good grass there."

Turon, who was normally a jokester, sensed John Stanley was in a somber mood.

"Everything all right, John Stanley?" Turon asked.

"Mister Hatcher offered me a job down south, breaking horses. Says he has a little house I can live in."

"Is that what you would like to do?" Turon studied the black cowboy.

"Yes sir, it is." John Stanley nodded.

"Are you going to take it?" Levi asked.

"I believe I will, Little Kansas."

"That's a good thing. Why do you act like someone shot your dog?" Turon asked.

"Well, Turon. I never thought I'd have my own house. Just figured I'd end up back in the cotton patch. I'll never pick cotton again." John Stanley nodded. "No sir, I'll never pick cotton again." He led the horses down to the creek bottom.

Turon and Levi walked to the house and stopped at the doorway.

Wes Hatcher leaned back in a chair at the table and peered through the doorway.

"Come on in. Chubb's got coffee."

Chubb was working at the wood range and set two mugs down on a wood plank table next to the stove. Filling the mugs with coffee he went back to work. The air in the room was overwhelming with smells of bread and the stovetop creations. A coal pit outside held several cast iron ovens that were roasting whole quails, a benefit of living and working on the tall grass prairie.

Turon and Levi removed their hats and took the mugs. Levi leaned against the wall and Turon squatted some distance away blowing steam from the hot mug.

Mr. Hatcher tested the ink on a letter he had just written to see if it had dried. Satisfied he folded the paper and set it on another folded letter.

"Turon, while I was in Caldwell I wrote and posted a letter on your behalf to Colonel Flemming in Canadian, Texas. I assume you're still interested in a Hereford bull?"

Turon lowered his coffee a little and looked surprised.

"Yes, sir, I am."

"Good, I thought you might be. I know you have put together a little herd back home in the Cherokee Nation. That prairie above Spring Creek where we picked up those yearlings last fall is prime country. If I were thirty years younger, I would marry a Cherokee girl and dig in."

"We could probably still find you a woman, Mr. Hatcher." Turon grinned.

"I'm sure you could, but my Beth would find out

and kill me sure as the sun comes up." Looking more serious he continued. "This big pasture ranching is over. Good seed bulls and growing bigger, fatter calves is the future. Flemming's Herefords are as good as you are going to find in the country. I intend to have some trailed to San Saba myself in the spring." Turning to Levi Mr. Hatcher changed his expression.

"How about you, Kuratowski? Still planning to open a store in Kansas City?"

Levi nodded. "Yes, sir, once I have enough money. A wagon first maybe until I have saved enough."

"It takes all kinds." Mr. Hatcher nodded. Handing a folded paper to Levi he continued. "It is not much but here is a letter of reference in case you ever need it. Also, if you choose to ride the train to Kansas City, look up Austin Petersen. He has a warehouse and freight yard. He may be able to help you in some way. He knows me and we have done a good deal of business together."

Blushing a little Levi took the letter.

"Thank you, Mr. Hatcher, this means a lot. Very thank you." The young immigrant tended to mix up his English when he got emotional.

Mr. Hatcher waved off his gratitude.

"Another year or two Levi, and you would make a cowhand. You will do well whatever line of work you choose."

The three visited long enough for Turon and Levi to drink the coffee.

"If you don't mind, could you have Ounce come see me?" Mr. Hatcher's request signaled the meeting was over. As the two finished off their coffee and began to leave Mr. Hatcher stopped them.

"Hold up, Turon, I've been meaning to ask. Is Ounce a nickname or his given name?" Mr. Hatcher knew Turon and Ounce were both from the same area.

"It is his given name. His mother said he was so little when he was born, he only weighed an ounce. So, they named him Ounce."

Mr. Hatcher knew a baby could not weigh an ounce and make it long, but he accepted the logic and the name.

"What kind of name is Turon?" Mr. Hatcher asked.

"I'm named after my mother's brother," Turon said simply.

"Your uncle's name is Turon? I have not heard the name before."

"His name is Ron," Turon said with a straight face.

"I thought you were named after him?"

"I was. See he's One Ron and I'm Two Ron."

Grinning Mr. Hatcher shook his head. "Go make yourself useful, fellas. Get on out of here."

In Cherokee Turon hailed Ounce as they approached the pen. Levi stood silent and tried to take in the language as the men conversed. It was as foreign to him as Yiddish would have been to the Cherokee cowboys.

Ounce nodded and walked toward the house. Turon and Levi walked to the shade of a Cottonwood tree. Preacher Bob sat silent with his eyes focused on putting an edge back on a knife while ignoring Frank who was doing most of the talking.

"I'm selling my saddle and outfit once I get to Caldwell. I'm through with chopping ice and pushing dumb animals from grass patch to grass patch," Frank said while the Boiling brothers sat nodding their approval.

"Little Kansas might need help clerking a store." Turon squatted near the base of the tree. "But I'm not sure he has room on the payroll for John and Jim."

Levi did not appreciate Turon casually bringing

him into Frank's rants. Frank had a streak of anger that lashed out often. Turon never seemed scared as some of the others and Frank never challenged him. Although after Turon's teasings, Frank sometimes went after nearby bystanders.

"Banking or maybe railroads," Frank said sternly. This surprised Levi. He never considered Frank the type to work in a bank or on a train for that matter.

"I knew you've been cowboying a long time Frank but didn't think you had saved enough money to open a bank." Turon grinned.

"Not working in a bank but robbing them. Jessie James and them Younger boys were on to something. These federals and banks are making too much off us little guys. Railroads just as bad," Frank said in a tone completely serious.

This did surprise Levi. Preacher Bob raised his head and stared at Frank. Turon grinned at the idea of Frank and the Boiling brothers robbing banks and trains. John Stanley walked up and squatted trying to follow the talk.

"Thou shalt not steal," Preacher Bob said simply.

"Bob, that is for neighbors and common folks. I am not talking about cattle, horses, or neighbors' wives. It is them federal folks and big money people. Look at the federals now. They are going to take this land from his people."

Frank continued while pointing a finger at Turon. "Just like they took my people's land in Tennessee and my mother's people's land in Ireland."

Levi who had seen his own family's land taken during a pogrom could not argue with Frank's statement. Neither could Turon. Turon's own people were forced from their homes and marched to the western lands assigned to them by the federal government.

Frank kept going. "They will open this land up for settlement soon. Cut it up into 160-acre tracts for anyone who wants it. Towns and railroads will take over. Then the bankers will own everything only to sell it to their friends for half the value. In twenty years, all the sod busters, pig men, and dairy farmers will be working to pay rent."

Preacher Bob was not able to hold his silence anymore. "Churches and schools will be here too. The plains will sprout a garden bringing a New Jerusalem."

"Well Bob, there will be a place for you I reckon. As far as me, I'm going to get what I can and strike for the Yukon." Frank stood up to stretch.

Turon studied a hole that was developing in his trouser leg and looked up at Frank.

"You better not let Mr. Hatcher hear you talking like this, Frank. He might not want an outlaw in the outfit. Besides, he keeps his money in banks," Turon said before turning his attention back to the trouser hole.

"Well, I'm just talking. One thing for sure. This country is going to change. It will never be the same once they drive off the cattle outfits." Frank showed a hint of sadness.

"You loafers come and get it. I will not holler twice," yelled Chubb.

In unison like a military unit the cowboys headed to the house. Chuck was on.

The morning after Mr. Hatcher's announcement the cowboys gathered what personal belongings they owned and destroyed the earthen shacks that had been home to them for several years. The dugout Turon and Levi shared had been built with what materials were at hand. It was big enough that it accommodated both men and occasionally Ounce as he stayed sometimes when delivering new strings of cow ponies.

Turon and Levi patrolled the boundary line along the Salt Fork and Arkansas Rivers where no fence had been erected. To have built a fence would have been futile due to spring floods. And a fence on high ground would have meant giving up grass along the river. South of the Salt Fork another cattle outfit had line riders who would push Hatcher cattle north across the river as Levi and Turon pushed their cattle back south. To the east lay the Osage Reservation. Hatcher did not mind his cattle crossing the Arkansas river provided his beef did not end up on an Osage table.

Levi had gathered what books he owned and was tying his bedroll onto a pack saddle Turon placed on a grey mare that was known to have some sense. In his bedroll was a spare set of clothes, tallit prayer cloth, and a single shot 16-gauge shotgun, a tool he used routinely to harvest quail and prairie chickens that supplemented their diet.

Turon likewise had his bedroll on the other side of the pack saddle. His too held most of his possessions including a hickory sprout bent double. Wrapped in rawhide, it held an eagle feather. Like Levi's prayer cloth, this feather held deep meaning. A change of clothes as well as a .45 caliber Henry rifle tucked into the center of the bedroll.

Both had India rubber slickers imported from a British company via Caldwell Mercantile and Dry Goods.

"Shame we have to knock it down." Levi turned to Turon who had tied a loop around the main roof beam.

Stepping into the saddle with the other end of the rope he nodded. "I agree, but Mr. Hatcher said we had to. Besides, old uton rattlesnake would just move in if we didn't."

Levi had learned enough Cherokee to know that

"uton" meant big.

Turon took a few wraps around the saddle horn and turned the bay away from the shack. With the rope tight the bay dropped his head and pulled against the weight of the structure. Before the rope could break, the main beam fell forward taking the door frame with it. The crash of timber and sod roof made the bay jump a little.

"Well, Little Kansas, there is no staying now. We are homeless."

Levi knew Turon was making a joke, but Levi was homeless. Stepping over to take the loop off the beam Levi looked at Turon who still sat on the bay coiling the slack in the rope.

"You going to Texas to buy a bull?" asked Levi as he slipped the loop off.

"I might as well. No more fun here. I figure after we get the cattle delivered, I will provision in Caldwell. Ounce will carry word home for me."

"I thought he might go south with Mr. Hatcher." Levi climbed aboard his horse.

"He offered Ounce a job. Ounce gets too homesick to move off far. Those Pathkillers like the woods. He has a girl on Cloud Creek he intends to marry. He was going to go home this fall anyway." Turon tied the rope onto his saddle string and looked at Levi. "You still set on Kansas City?"

"Yeah, I think so." Levi leaned from the saddle catching up the lead rope to the roan mare.

Turon tilted his hat back on his head. "There is a need for peddlers and store clerks in the Nation. Cherokee City on the line has horse races every Saturday. Row has a hotel. Tahlequah for sure is better than Kansas City. If peddling does not pan out, you can always cowboy for day work. Least you will not starve."

Levi pondered on that. Turon had made this case

before.

"If Kansas City does not work, then maybe I come find you," Levi said.

"You do that." Looking around at the ruins of the dugout Turon asked, "You ready?"

"Ya, let's go."

An afternoon sun shined down on Turon and Levi as they rode back into Hatcher's headquarters. Chubb and John Stanley were outfitting the chuckwagon and the wood range had been moved outside. Mr. Hatcher intended on hauling it back to Texas. He was known to be generous while in season but would not give a stove like that away nor sell it at a loss. Along with the stove an anvil sat on a crosscut section of log. These items would be picked up on the return trip from Caldwell then hauled south.

Preacher Bob had agreed to drive the spare wagon and help with the move. John Stanley would trail the horses leaving Chubb with the chuckwagon. Frank and the Boiling brothers had no plans to go to Texas although they helped move items from the house.

Supper time came and most of everything was in order. Mr. Hatcher addressed them all after each had a plate.

"Frank, I think it best if we split up in the morning. I want you to take Bob and the Boiling brothers. From the rock crossing ride up the Salt Fork. Spread out and make a sweep up to the line fence. Watch for fresh tracks along the river. Any sign of our cattle crossing south, find them. Push everything north to that lightning struck cottonwood on Cowskin Creek. That's where Chubb will make camp. John Stanley will take the horses with him."

Frank nodded. "Yes sir, Mr. Hatcher."

"I will take Turon, Ounce, and Little Kansas and make a sweep north along the Arkansas. Anything we find we'll push to the Cowskin."

None of the men on this crew asked questions. They each knew what their job entailed.

"The day after we'll sweep north and leave a few of us with the herd so they don't drift. Then we'll get a count and cut out any cow brute that is not a Hatcher beef animal. Depending on the count, if we need to, we'll make another sweep."

The crew sat patiently waiting in silence for Mr. Hatcher to finish speaking.

"Once the count is satisfied, we will keep to the south bank of the Chikaskia. Follow it up to the quarantine grounds. The buyer will take possession of the herd there."

Mr. Hatcher stood, but before walking away, said, "Eat up, gentlemen. We've got a good deal of work tomorrow."

CHAPTER 4

————◆«◆»◆————

The day before the buyer was to take possession the Hatcher crew drove the herd onto the quarantine grounds south of Caldwell, Kansas. Livestock inspectors had looked for signs of tick fever and checked brands before allowing the animals into the state of Kansas.

The cowboys were on horseback up wind from the cattle waiting for Mr. Hatcher and the new owner to finish looking the herd over. Chubb had already packed up the chuckwagon and headed into town across the line that separated Kansas and the Cherokee Outlet. John Stanley, with help from Ounce, had driven the spare horses to a wagon yard on the south side of town.

"Looks like they're in agreement," Frank said while Mr. Hatcher shook hands with the buyer.

"That's it then," Preacher Bob said softly.

"When do we get to go into town?" asked John.

"Yeah, I'm ready to see a woman." Jim's eyes widened.

"Why? Your mother in town?" Turon joked between puffs of a cigarette.

Both John and Jim's faces reddened as laughter flared up among the cowboys. They had both been thinking of the Pleasant House, a residence on the edge of town near the stockyards.

"Not unless Fat Fannie is their mother." Frank chuckled. "You boys best stick with me and avoid that place. If you don't catch critters, you'll catch the drip."

Embarrassed, both John and Jim tried to appear small in their saddles. Wishing they had not brought it up, mainly because they could not get the image out of their mind of their mother engaging in the occupation that occurred at the Pleasant House.

Mr. Hatcher left the buyer and rode toward the cowboys. He reined his horse to a stop and faced the semi-circle of men that moved closer within earshot.

"Deal's done, boys. Littlefield's Wagon Yard is expecting you. Chubb will have your gear. I'll be there at two o'clock to pay you off." Mr. Hatcher gave the Boiling brothers a stern look. "Try not to burn the town down before I get my wagon and horses out. See you at two."

Frank was the oldest of the crew, but his exuberance contrasted Preacher Bob's somberness. Frank let out a shout—part Rebel yell and part Comanche war cry. A sound so loud that Preacher Bob's horse crow hopped nearly dumping the pious cowboy to the ground. Spurring his horse into a run Frank led a race toward town with the Boiling brothers close behind.

The rest of the crew held back. They were not as excited as the other three to see town, and Mr. Hatcher still owned the horses they rode.

"He will never learn. Dead broke in a week I'll wager and the other two will not have six bits between them." Mr. Hatcher shook his head. "You boys behave yourselves."

The wagon yard offered some protection from the elements and a refuge for cowboys. Shade in the summer and a good stove in the office during the winter. Unless conditions proved to be too severe most cowboys even slept at the wagon yard, finding it preferable to the crowded hotel beds.

The crew waited in the shade. Most had been to the dining hall. Turon, Ounce, Levi, and John Stanley took their meals on the porch of the dinning hall. No matter how Mr. Hatcher treated them or other drovers, townspeople were sometimes quick to judge them based on the shade of their skin. In Levi's case it was when he spoke.

The wagon yard held no prejudices, however. The black John Stanley sat beside Preacher Bob laughing at some observation they shared. The Jewish Levi played dominoes on a saddle blanket with the two Cherokees, Turon and Ounce.

Frank walked up followed by the brothers. The three smelled faintly of beer. They had finished off sandwiches and hop drinks at the German house down the street. Although the state of Kansas had prohibition on alcohol people still managed to find a drink. Loopholes in the law like private clubs with cheap membership dues allowed people to find drinks.

Soon Mr. Hatcher appeared from around the corner carrying a leather wallet and stack of papers. Chubb walked beside him with a bulge under his coat that the cowboys knew would be an army revolver, a Civil War relic re-chambered for cartridges.

A barrel stood nearby, and Mr. Hatcher used it as a desk. He set the leather wallet down and placed a rock on the stack of papers.

"Let's get on with it. Frank, are you picking a horse or you want the forty dollars?"

"I'll take the money, Mr. Hatcher. I'm heading out on the next train." Frank faced the old rancher.

Mr. Hatcher handed Frank his wages and the two

shook hands.

"Frank, you are a top hand. If you're ever down San Saba way, I might be able to find a place for you."

"Thank you for that offer but I am bound for the Yukon."

"Be careful you don't end up as bear bait." Mr. Hatcher was not joking.

As Frank turned away the Boiling brothers stepped side by side to the barrel.

"How about you two? Horses or forty dollars?"

John spoke first then Jim. Both wanted the money. Mr. Hatcher handed them cash, and they went to stand by Frank.

"See you boys around town. I'll be at the German House if you want a drink." Frank walked off followed by the brothers.

John Stanley and Preacher Bob only took a little spending money since they were still on the payroll. Neither required much in the way of entertainment funds. Preacher Bob did not partake in night life, and any establishment would not have welcomed John.

Ounce picked out a black gelding for which Mr. Hatcher gave him a bill of sale along with his wages. Levi, who had intentions of going to Kansas City on the train, collected his wages and shook the hand of the man who had given him an opportunity where others had turned him away.

Turon stepped forward.

"I will take the bay if that's all right with you, Mr. Hatcher."

"Suits me fine." Mr. Hatcher wrote the horse's description on the bill of sale.

"Since Little Kansas did not want a pony, how would you like to trade for that hammer headed pinto?" Turon asked while jerking his thumb toward the horses in the lot.

"There's better horses than that in the bunch." Mr. Hatcher nodded toward the lot.

"I like him. He reminds me of a wolf hound I once had." Turon said while scratching behind his right ear.

"Twenty dollars, and I'll add him to the bill of sale." Mr. Hatcher waited.

Turon shoved his hand forward and the two shook on it.

"A wolf hound, huh?" Mr. Hatcher wrote the pinto's description on the bill of sale.

"Oh yeah, he will make a good night horse too."

"Night horse?" Mr. Hatcher's eyes squinted.

"Those white spots will show up at night in the moonlight. If I can see him that means the rest of the horses are still there," Turon said.

Smiling Mr. Hatcher shook Turon's hand again and gave him the bill of sale and his wages.

"Mr Chubb, how about a drink at the Drover's before we leave town?" Mr. Hatcher and Chubb left the wagon yard and walked to the Drover's Hotel and the adjacent tavern.

Turon and Ounce spoke to each other in Cherokee for a few minutes as Levi stood by listening but not understanding very much. The Cherokee turned to English and Turon looked at Levi.

"Ounce is going to leave this afternoon for the Territory. He does not care for town. You know how them Indians are," Turon said while Ounce stood grinning. "I am going to leave too. As soon as I get some supplies from the mercantile."

Turon started to say more but a man on a dapple-gray gelding rode into the wagon yard and hollered for the stable hand to come put his horse away. Pitching the stable hand a few coins as he dismounted, the man started to leave the wagon yard but stopped to look over the three cowboys.

Turning to Levi the man spoke. "What cow outfit are you with?"

Levi replied. "Hatcher, from down in the Outlet."

"How many of you are in town?" The man asked.

The three knew who he was by the badge pinned to a leather flap on his coat chest pocket. As a city marshal, he kept the peace and enforced city ordinances. His reputation among the cowhands of the area was more of a head thumper. Many a drunken cowboy woke up with a headache not caused by alcohol.

Levi replied again. "Eight total."

"Mind you behave yourselves while in town." The marshal walked out into the street toward the town center.

Ounce spoke in Cherokee and Turon answered. The stable hand appeared from the shadows.

"That's Marshal Colcord. I heard he was getting a commission to be a U.S. Marshal. Hate to see him go. He tips good. He cracks a few skulls but only those who earn it." The stable hand returned to cleaning the stalls.

"Ounce said he's going to get the horses ready. He asked me to get a few things for him. Need anything from the store?" Turon asked Levi.

Levi did not need much, and it could wait. But he was not ready to see his friend go yet so he accompanied Turon to the town center and offered to carry items. Turon would not come across any towns on his way to Canadian, Texas. After stopping at the bank to close his account he bought the basics— cartridges, flour, and salt as well as some treats. Canned peaches, hard candy, a canvas tarp, and rope completed his order, and the two carried the items to the wagon yard.

Ounce had his new black horse saddled as well as Turon's bay and pinto, the one with the makeshift pack saddle. The cowboys divided the goods, Ounce's being less for he intended to travel fast.

Stuffing his part into a canvas sack Ounce bounded into the saddle, spoke briefly in Cherokee, then turned to Levi.

"Little Kansas, come see me sometime. Watch out for the Yonega." With that Ounce Pathkiller walked his horse through the wagon yard gate and rode out of town.

"What's a Yonega?" asked Levi.

Turon smiled. "White man. There's a bunch up in Kansas City."

Turon took his time loading the pinto with the supplies. The horse watched him and eyed the load.

"You should come with me," Turon said while tying the canvas tarp on top of the pack.

In a way Levi wanted to go with the Cherokee cowboy. He had a sense of dread most of the afternoon. He was not sure if it was the chance he may never see his friend again or if it was the idea of starting something new.

"You have your dream. I have mine. I do not have enough for both a wagon and trade goods. Maybe in Kansas City I will have enough in a year," Levi said.

"Kansas City will always be there. You should give Indian Territory a try. Missouri and Kansas both have all the stores they need."

Levi smiled and nodded. "You should stay the night. John Stanley says it will rain."

Sniffing the air like a hound Turon nodded. "It might. Even more reason for me to get out of town. Towns are too sloppy when it rains."

Turon tightened the cinch on the bay then stuck his hand out and Levi took it.

"Goodbye," Levi said with some sadness.

"The Cherokee do not have a word for goodbye. So,

I will see you later." Turon stepped into the saddle and Levi handed him the pinto's lead rope. "If you change your mind, I intend to take the Wagon Road south then up the Canadian River to the Flemming's Ranch."

"Good luck," Levi said.

Nodding Turon urged the bay out onto the street with the pinto following as Levi watched his friend ride south. The burden of the pinto pack bounced as he kicked at a passing town dog that got too close. Soon they were lost in wagon traffic and Levi stood alone still staring south.

CHAPTER 5

———◆«◆»◆———

The afternoon sky darkened as clouds rolled in from the west. Levi moved down the timbered sidewalk pausing to look through windows. Seeing his reflection in the glass he debated if he should buy a new hat. His was suited for the prairies but soon he would be looking for work in the city. Before he could step inside to look at the hats, a voice hailed him.

"Little Kansas! Join us for a drink," Frank called out with the Boiling brothers in tow.

Frank was in good spirits and the brothers walked with a liquid swagger.

"Rude folks at the German House. A farmer got smart-mouthed, and John here had to tune him up a bit." Frank waved a hand toward John Boiling as he puffed his chest out.

"Will there be trouble?" Levi asked.

"None that we can't handle." Frank slapped Levi on the back turning him in the direction they traveled.

Reluctant, Levi joined the cowboys to the Drover's Tavern.

"Maybe just one drink before supper," Levi offered.

"Skip supper and drink it instead." Frank let out a big laugh.

As the three entered the tavern Levi looked around hoping to see Mr. Hatcher or someone he knew. He liked Frank and the brothers, but he preferred to go unnoticed in a crowd. With the loud Frank and laughing brothers, they were attracting too much attention. Frank ordered drinks and slapped a paper note on the bar, letting the bartender know he intended to spend it all.

"There he is, Marshal. That's the cowboy." A man in overalls pointed at John.

The cowboys turned as Marshal Colcord moved from the man's side and stepped toward the bar. John looked dumbfounded and frozen in confusion.

"You other three step aside. Boy, put that drink down and step over here." The marshal's voice was heavy with authority.

Placing the drink down John stepped forward obeying the command.

"Do you have a gun on your person, boy?"

John shook his head no and confusion started to give way to irritation. Levi tried to look small and innocent, which was not hard for the 5-foot 2-inch immigrant.

"You are under arrest for assault, battery, and disturbing the peace. Stay calm and come with me. Yeoman here pays taxes. We cannot have vagrants roughing up the tax base."

John looked at Frank who belligerently stepped toward to the marshal.

"Now wait one minute. That pig jockey started it." Frank defiantly pointed at the short heavy farmer.

"Sir, get back. You can make a statement tomorrow morning." The marshal blocked his way.

"No. I'll make it now." Frank abruptly stepped forward.

If Frank had seen the marshal slip the leather-wrapped lead weight out of a pocket, he did not pay it any mind. As if swatting a fly, the marshal struck Frank a glancing blow that knocked him to his knees where he crumbled over.

Jim charged the marshal and would have met a well-timed blow to the head if John had not stepped in just in time and hit the distracted marshal in the jaw. The hardheaded Frank came to action kicking the legs out from under the marshal sending him to the floor and Frank's level.

Filled with rage Frank delivered several hard-knuckled hits and stood up over the marshal's limp body. Reaching for the leather thumper Frank bounced it in his hand.

"You won't use this anymore to thump folks." Frank looked down at the marshal who was still limp.

As an afterthought Frank bent over and took the revolver tucked into the marshal's waistband.

"I don't think I want you shooting me in the back either."

Having seen it all unfold in a matter of seconds; Levi rushed forward to protest. Before he could say anything, the farmer Yeoman ran out of the tavern into the street.

"Murder! They are murdering the marshal," yelled the farmer.

The quick acting Frank yanked Levi and shoved him toward the door. "We got to go."

Panic overcame Levi and he ran with the others to the wagon yard. In a rush Frank grabbed his saddle that he previously intended to sell and quickly began saddling a sorrel that was in a stall. The stable hand came out of the office and began to protest.

"What's going on here?" He was all a fluster.

"We're borrowing these horses," Frank snapped.

"The hell you are." The stable hand started to

intervene and grab the horse's reins.

Frank pulled the lawman's revolver from his own waistband and thrust it in the direction of the stable hand.

"You'd best take a walk," Frank said sternly.

The stable hand backed away and soon was running through the gate out into the street.

"Better saddle up, Little Kansas." Frank finished saddling the horse.

"I did nothing wrong." Levi's face reddened.

"You're a cowboy and you ran. These folks won't care. Grab a saddle. That gray looks like he can run." Frank motioned to the dapple gray the marshal had rode into the wagon yard earlier.

"I'm innocent," Levi continued.

"Either ride with us now or you'll rot in jail," Frank replied.

The Boiling brothers each mounted a horse. Frank pulled a saddle and blanket from a rack and shoved it into Levi's arms. With the gray saddled Levi hastily tied on his bedroll and gear. He grabbed a bridle that fit the gray.

"Let's go!" Frank shouted.

People were gathering and men shouted. At seventeen hands, the gray was stout in build. Levi and his gear were no burden, and the horse could run. Frank led the way and headed to the river crossing. Once across, Frank slowed and took a southeast direction toward the Outlet. Thunder rolled and lightning flashed on the horizon to the west.

"What do we do now?" asked John.

"We go on the scout. Best thing we can do is go to the Nations. We'll provision in Pawhuska. Then maybe the Creek or Choctaw Nation. No one back there knew us except our outfit. Doubt they'd say anything." Frank glanced back to see if they were being followed.

Levi's sense of dread made him sick. His determination to do right overtook his fear to disappoint Frank.

"I am going back," Levi said while turning the gray around.

Frank whirled and cut him off blocking his path.

"Go back and do what?" He was angry. "You stole a horse. You were with us when we thumped the marshal. If he dies, you'll swing. If he does not die, they will whip you before locking you in a rock quarry."

Levi was frustrated with Frank and himself. "Like you said, they do not know us. I will get close enough to let the horse loose. I will walk to Kansas City, by God."

"Too bad you don't have brains to match that hard head, you sawed off kike." Frank reined his horse out of Levi's way. "Good luck."

With that Frank and the Boiling brothers left Levi on the trail as the gray pranced wanting to go with the other horses.

Levi rode back toward town thinking of the best way to get the horse back to the wagon yard. He had decided as soon as he was in sight of the town he would just step out of the saddle, unload his gear, and slap the horse on the rump. Being a horse accustomed to oats and hay at the wagon yard the horse would naturally return on its own, leaving Levi to walk the prairie and avoid people until this whole event blew over.

Thunder continued to rumble, and lighting flashed in the distance. The slicker was in his bedroll, and he would get it out as soon as he set the gray free. It was while thinking of this that Levi noticed the approaching riders.

He stopped the horse and watched the men. It was clear they had seen him. A dozen men all carrying rifles or shotguns. Levi felt dread again but was determined that he could explain the situation. They were less than two hundred yards away when he started to step out of the saddle to surrender.

Two thuds and two clouds of dust exploded on either side of him and the horse, followed quickly by two loud gunshots. Three more clouds of dust erupted around him as bullets ripped into the earth. Levi saw a man waving and yelling at the others, but the noise was all lost in the thunder that sounded right on top of him.

"Shit." Levi shouted and turned the gray south away from the approaching riders.

He did not need to spur the horse that leaped into a run as Levi lowered himself in the saddle trying to make for a smaller target. Lightning struck nearby sending the gray into breakneck speed. Rain started with big drops that pelted and stung Levi. He pulled his hat down low, and the drops turned torrential.

Levi rode blind keeping the horse headed south the best he could. After what seemed like a mile, he slowed his mount as the rain slowed. He could not see anyone following him. He could not see anything really. Still, he rode on. Everything he owned was wet. Darkness had not come yet, but the storm was not letting up.

Well into the Outlet he heard the roar of water and debris come rushing downstream as he crossed Deer Creek. Drumming his heels into the sides of the gray he urged him across and onto higher ground.

He paused and watched the torrent roll past carrying trees, grass, and mud.

"No one will cross that for a while," he said aloud.

Keeping a watch to the north he let the gray rest. It was dark when he tightened the cinch and swung into the saddle. Southward he rode and the stars shone bright. Still wet from the storm he shivered in the night air.

Levi weighed his options. He would not find Frank

who said they were on the scout which meant dodging the law. They would cover their tracks and lose themselves in a country Frank knew well.

The town of Caldwell was out. Levi would not show himself to another trigger-happy citizen of that town. Even if he proved himself innocent of beating the law officer, he would more than likely hang for stealing the gray.

Levi was tired. He had ridden all night and the sun was up. Its warmth was a comfort and, although hungry, what he needed was sleep and a clear mind so he could decide what to do. Finding a spot where a cottonwood grew near a rock ledge facing south Levi spread out his belongings to dry. After rubbing the gray down, he used some rope from his sack of gear and staked the horse out where he could graze. Stretching out on his slicker he covered his face with his hat, the scent of his own sweat from the hat brim filling his nostrils. He soon fell asleep.

CHAPTER 6

———◆❝◆❞◆———

Levi stood in a store and watched people coming in to buy goods. He pulled items off a shelf only to drop them, and the annoyed customers disappeared. This kept happening over and over. Outside the store the rain fell and soon his roof was leaking. All his goods were getting soaked, and water was rising all around him. He could not understand what caused the leak but soon discovered men shooting holes in the roof.

The sound of a horse stomping his hoof woke Levi from his dream and he stretched. He vaguely wondered if his boots were dry. Then remembering the horse, he realized it was too close and must have pulled up its stake.

Removing his hat, Levi stared into the bright sunlight and a silhouette of a man sitting horseback sent fear rushing through him. Jumping up half-crouched he was so quick that the man's horse startled.

"Siyo, Little Kansas, you have a poor camp." Turon grinned at the half-frightened immigrant.

"I am glad to see you." Levi sighed with relief.

Turon pulled a cold roasted quail from a sack and tossed it to Levi who caught it and talked while he ate. He told about the run-in with the marshal and the escape that took place soon after.

"You're too nervous to make an outlaw and too easy to catch," Turon said. "Better come with me."

"What if they catch us and we have that horse?" Levi asked.

"We will cross that creek when we get there," Turon said eyeing the gray. "Put your gear and bedroll on the pinto. We will cut west through the leases and avoid the wagon road. They will not look for you out west. They will think you headed south or east."

Levi started gathering his gear and belongings now dried by the sun.

"I doubt Frank killed that marshal. That was him shouting at the rest of them not to shoot his horse when they took after you more than likely."

This made Levi feel better.

"What about the horse?" Levi asked.

Turon looked the gray over again. "I do not see any brand on him. No marks easily stand out. I say we brand him. You can send that marshal fifty dollars one day when you get a chance. Just do not sign your real name to the letter."

This idea appealed to Levi, and Turon built a small fire and pulled a spare cinch ring from his pack and placed it in the fire. Since they had a fire Turon retrieved a recent purchase from the pinto's pack. A small Goodrich coffee percolator.

"Since we have a fire, might as well have some coffee," Turon said.

The two waited for the coffee to boil and the cinch ring to heat up.

"What brand do you want?" Turon asked. "I can put my brand on him if you cannot think of one."

Levi thought it best not to involve his friend in larceny.

"I don't know," Levi looked toward the gray horse.

"It can be a number, does not have to be a symbol."

Levi thought of this and thought back to his days in Cheder long ago and the teacher from his home village.

"Forty then," Levi said.

"Forty?" Turon questioned while checking the red-hot cinch ring.

"Yes."

"Forty it is," Turon said.

To "throw" a horse was a phrase not a practice. The two used ropes and gently laid the gray down on its side and restrained him so he would not kick or get up. Turon then used two sticks and pulled the red-hot cinch ring from the fire. With Levi holding the head and neck of the horse down Turon burned the number forty down low on the gray's forearm.

"He'll be forty below from now on." Turon walked to the pinto's pack and retrieved a tin container. He fingered some tallow out and slathered it on the fresh brand before letting the gray get up. If the gray horse resented the alteration to his hide, he did not show it. As soon as the cinch ring was cool to the touch, Turon stuffed it into his sack of gear.

With the gray's identity established the two cowboys rode west avoiding leases where they might know the cowhands. With each mile they passed, the odds of someone recognizing them diminished. After two days Levi was more at ease.

The two-rode side by side as they approached a salt plain. Levi had heard of the great deposit of salt but had never seen it.

"It's like a different country." Levi watched the heat waves dance across the barren landscape.

"For hundreds of years tribes from all over came here to get salt," Turon said.

Turon had been curious about the brand Levi had chosen. Finally, he had to ask.

"Why forty for the brand?"

"I had a teacher that taught me numbers had special meanings. The number forty throughout the Torah stands for change, renewal, or a new beginning."

Turon did not reply so Levi continued. "After Noah built the ark, it rained for forty days and forty nights. Moses fasted for forty days and forty nights to receive the law."

"The Cherokee have their special numbers. The four directions on earth. Seven for the seven clans of the Cherokee," Turon said.

The two cowboys rode on; each one separated from their own tribe. One by only a couple hundred miles. One by thousands. More alike in their own ways than different.

"Let us hope we do not spend forty years wandering the wilderness. We ain't got time for that," Turon said while turning to check the pinto.

They had ridden beyond the salt outcrop and were in low sand hills when Turon spotted two columns of riders approaching from the northwest.

"Soldiers," he said.

Nervously Levi looked toward the blue uniformed men. "We could get below this hill and maybe they won't see us." He scanned behind them.

"Why? We ain't done nothing wrong. Just cattlemen on business to Texas to buy a bull." Turon sounded slightly irritated.

The nervous Levi relaxed some, and they waited for the soldiers who were riding directly toward them. The soldiers reined up thirty yards from them on command from a lieutenant at the head of the troop. Riding closer to the cowboys the lieutenant stopped and addressed them.

"Afternoon, gentlemen." He looked them over especially Turon.

"What can we do for you?" Turon asked.

"I am Lieutenant Lafferty. We are looking for boomers and squatters. I assume you are with one of these cow outfits?"

"Was. We are headed to the Flemming's Ranch to pick up a bull to trail back to the Cherokee Nation." Turon said while adjusting himself in the saddle.

"I see," said Lieutenant Lafferty. "Colonel Flemming is well known. I have heard stories of his Comanche campaigns. I understand at West Point they teach about his route at Glorieta Pass."

"He has good bulls is all I know about him." Turon stood in the stirrups and stretched.

"Brought in stock from Illinois several years back." Lieutenant Lafferty looked the cowboys up and down. "Least that's what I have heard."

"Anything we should know about the trail between here and Canadian?" Turon asked.

"It's dry between the Cimarron and Canadian rivers. Unless you know where the springs are, you better pack some water." Lieutenant Lafferty eyed the pack on the pinto. "You say you are going to trail a bull from Canadian to the Cherokee Nation?" The lieutenant's head raised as he appraised them.

"We were going to ship him on a steamboat, but we could not afford the freight," Turon said straight-faced.

Lieutenant Lafferty not accustomed to having an Indian speak so witty and direct to him and turned to Levi. "Does he work for you or are you both on business for your boss?"

Levi spoke for the first time. "He's the boss. I'm just here to help."

The lieutenant had heard stories of wealthy Cherokees. Rogers was a name well known along with his Dog Iron Ranch.

"I see. The reason I asked, is you better keep a close eye on your bull. If he strays, a Cheyenne may help himself to a beef steak and jerk the rest," the lieutenant said.

After glancing back at his men, the lieutenant bid farewell and wished Turon and Levi good luck. Turning his horse, he called out.

"Sergeant, move them out."

As the soldiers rode past, Turon turned to Levi who looked visibly relieved.

"Little Kansas, you have to stop looking like you just stole the sugar sack."

Levi shifted in the saddle and watched the departing soldiers. "It wasn't you who got shot at the other day," he said.

"Who among us hasn't been shot at time to time?" Turon said with a sweep of his arm.

Levi said nothing to that. He had only been on the American prairies for two years so maybe it was normal having people shoot at you.

Turon studied his hand and counted silently with his fingers.

"Tomorrow is Saturday." Turon looked at Levi then asked, "When is the last time you took a Shabbat?"

Levi thought on it. It had been too long since he honored the Sabbath. Sundays were typically slow days for the cowboys. Saturdays were working days on the range. Rarely had Levi routinely practiced his faith since arriving on the prairies.

"Too long," he simply said.

"Well, the horses could use a rest. It might be a dry stretch between the rivers. We will find a place before dark and rest tomorrow," Turon said.

Levi became overwhelmed by gratitude. "Thank you."

"Think nothing of it. While the horses graze you can get your mind right."

CHAPTER 7

————◆"◆"◆————

The land they now traveled through was drier than the tall grass in the eastern part of the Outlet. They rode until they came across a little grove of trees along a spring-fed creek. A waist-deep pool of water stood beneath a rock outcropping.

"Plenty of wood and water," Turon said.

Levi nodded. "Looks like a good place to camp."

"Why don't you take care of the pinto and gray and make camp?" Turon checked the chamber of the Henry rifle. He had started carrying the rifle on his saddle in hopes of seeing a deer or antelope. "I will have a look around. See if I can get us some camp meat." He left Levi to his work.

This was to Levi's favor. One crucial step in the Jewish Shabbat was cleaning and tidying up the home. For the time being their home was this camp along the creek. Levi quickly tied the canvas tarp into a lean-to after he watered, rubbed down, and staked the horses. He cleared a spot, built a small fire, and gathered enough wood for the night and next day.

Unrolling his bedroll, he took fresh clothes and laid them out along with his tallit prayer cloth. Once he had all in order, he retrieved a bar of soap from his gear bag.

Removing his boots and hat he started to the creek. Remembering his knife, he stopped and put it in the hat along with some money and other items he did not want wet. Wading into the water he used the soap to wash his clothes and himself in preparation for his day of rest.

Naked, Levi carried his wet clothes to some low hanging branches. While dressing in his spare set of clothes he heard a gunshot some distance away. Levi listened. Another shot came a few seconds later. Both sounded like meat shots. Levi had become accustomed to how gunshots sounded. Turon who rarely missed or fired into the air always brought meat back that matched his shots. Levi was decent with his shotgun, but Turon was a sharpshooter.

By the time he was in fresh clothes, Turon rode into camp. Two turkeys hung on either side of his saddle horn.

"I know where they are roosting. We can have more when we head out Sunday," Turon said stepping down from the saddle.

Levi took the birds downstream and began dressing them while Turon unsaddled his horse. Coming back to camp Levi hung the carcasses on a limb.

"We can roast one now and mud the other one, and it will be ready for tomorrow," Turon said.

Sunset was approaching as one turkey was roasting over the fire split into two halves. Levi had dug a hole near the fire according to Turon's instructions. Meanwhile Turon was on the edge of the creek where he had salted and seasoned the second turkey. After stuffing it with some cattail roots, he packed wet clay and switchgrass around the whole bird until it resembled a large pumpkin.

Levi gathered rocks as Turon had instructed and

placed them at the bottom of the hole.

"That is enough, Little Kansas. You are about out of daylight." Turon set the mud caked turkey aside. "I'll stick this one in the hole in the morning and it will be ready by dinner time tomorrow."

"Thank you for this," Levi said.

"It is nothing, we ain't in no hurry. The horses need the rest. We do too." Turon pulled a tobacco pouch from his pocket. "What else do we need to do?" Turon looked at the sun beginning its descent.

"It is time to light a candle. But I have no candles. The fire will be fine though." Levi smiled.

Turon walked over to his gear bag and pulled out a candle from his pack that he kept while traveling.

"Here you go, one just like it saved me once during a snowstorm. I always travel with a couple ever since." Turon handed a candle to the surprised Levi.

Levi was overjoyed. He held the bottom of the candle to a coal to soften the wax. Once soft he placed it on a rock sticking it in place.

"Now I light the candle," Levi pulled a burning stick from the fire.

Turon could appreciate the rituals Levi honored. In a way it was much like his own, his being a mix of Cherokee and Christian practices. Everything special had a song. Every action a reason. Although Levi's faith was different, Turon respected it.

Turon turned the turkey halves over and tested with his knife to see how cooked they were. "Should not be much longer."

"This is about the time we would sing the Shalom Aleichem and Eshet and Hayil." Levi paused. "Do you mind if I sing?"

"Do whatever you need to do. Let me know if I need to do something."

Levi spoke in a language Turon could not

understand. Then he started to sing.
"Shalom aleichem
mal'achei ha-sharet
mal'achei Elyon,
mi-melech malchei
ha-milachim
ha-kadosh Baruch Hu."

Turon listened to what he thought were four more verses of the song. He could not understand a word. As he watched Levi sing and slowly rock forward and back a thought came to him. *This is the strangest white man I have ever come across.*

Levi stopped singing.

"There is a second song. The Eshet and Hayil. It is about women of valor. How a wife must have honor."

"The Cherokee have similar songs. Our Beloved Women, we call them," Turon said.

He then listened to Levi sing the Eshet and Hayil. Again, he could not understand any of it but felt as moved as he had ever been hearing a hymn or chant. Levi finished and indicated that was all of the song.

"When do we eat?" Turon asked.

"Now, if it is ready." Levi nodded.

Using knives the two sliced off portions of the roasting turkey. They ate and shared stories. Above them a multitude of stars illuminated the sky.

The next morning Levi walked to a little hill and sat thinking about how fortunate he had been to have a friend like Turon. When he first came to America and then the west, he had been scared to meet an Indian. Now he preferred the company of Turon and Ounce. Frank had nearly gotten him killed. It was on these thoughts that he turned to prayer.

Turon too was up early. He checked the horses letting Levi pray and be alone. Afterwards he shoveled coals from the fire into the hole Levi dug the previous night. He checked the mud-wrapped turkey. Placing the mud ball on the coals and rocks he shoveled more coals around and on top of the turkey, finally covering it all with about three inches of dirt.

Turon then walked over to his gear and pulled out the rawhide-wrapped container that held a single eagle's feather. Removing the feather, he ran his fingers along its edge. With this Turon walked away from camp past the horses. Near a giant cedar along the creek, he performed his own religious ceremony, the feather as significant as the tallit. The songs carrying the same weight. Then he knelt in prayer.

By noon they dug up the turkey. The mud had turned black and set up like a brick. Using the short-handled shovel Turon tapped the caked mud ball. Cracking it like a giant egg he split it into halves and watched steam escape into the air. The meat fell from the bone and cattail roots resembled potatoes. They ate, surprised by how tender it was. Levi nodded approvingly at the taste in his mouth.

"This is good." he said between bites."

"Old Indian trick. Works good with fish," Turon said.

"Do you think there is opportunity where you are from for a store?" Levi asked.

"If you trade fair, most Cherokee rather not cross the line," Turon said. "You could have goods shipped to Siloam Springs, Arkansas on the train. Load them up on a wagon and go west into the Nation. Set up a camp like this and sell out in a week."

"Then, that is what I will do." Levi nodded.

Levi did not do any of the idle work that downtime in cowboy culture entailed. His socks needed mending and his clothes from the previous day still hung on limbs. Dry now but continuing to air out. After lunch he stretched out to take a nap.

Turon decided he should do some laundry as well and take advantage of the creek. He too walked into the creek clothed with a bar of soap. Scrubbing his clothes he peeled off in layers until he was down to his own hide. Once finished he hung his clothes to dry and changed into ones he had laid out.

Sundown ended Levi's Shabbat, and he went about gathering more wood and tended the gray horse in the dark, leading him to the creek for a chance to water. By early the next morning they rode out after having coffee and another turkey hung from the pinto's pack saddle.

CHAPTER 8

———————◆«◆»◆———————

Riding southwest they crossed the Cimarron River and Lieutenant Lafferty had been correct. Coming to the North Canadian River they had to dig holes in the sandy river bottom and wait for water to seep in. They dug holes for the horses and one for themselves to get water for coffee.

Crossing the military road that ran between Fort Supply and Fort Reno they saw several tracks from what they assumed were army patrols looking for boomers and squatters that routinely tried to penetrate what they considered open and free land.

Near where the Great Western Trail crossed the Canadian River, they came across a cattle herd. Driving the herd were cowboys from the Day Brothers Cattle Company.

"We're taking heifers back to Texas. Too dry for them up here," a raw-boned cowboy said.

Levi remembered the monsoon rain that nearly drowned him less than two weeks before. *If only we could have spread it around.*

"Cook's wagon is down by the river if y'all want to stay for supper," the cowboy offered.

"Much obliged." Turon nodded.

"It's nothing." The cowboy said before yelling a command in Spanish to a passing vaquero. "See you at the wagon." He spurred his horse to help the vaquero bring a roan heifer back into the herd.

The cook was a short man who spoke Spanish when he offered coffee to Turon and Levi. Turon had picked up a little Spanish over the years, but he could not carry a conversation very far. Accepting the coffee, they visited a little. The cook switched to English once he learned the bronze-skinned Turon could not speak Spanish very well.

"I am called Claudio. Picket your horses. We will eat soon," said the cook whose Indio tan was as dark as Turon's.

Riders came in one at a time. All were careful not to stir up dust as they approached the cocinero's domain. Half the crew were Anglos and the rest Mexican cowboys. All used Spanish intertwined with English. The cowboy who had invited them to the wagon turned out to be the foreman.

"My name is Tom Pogue. I'm the foreman for the Day Brothers."

Shaking hands Turon introduced himself. Levi stepped forward and did likewise.

"Is it dry back east?"

"It had been dry, not as dry as here. They got a good rain when we left Caldwell. Any news out of Canadian, Texas?" Turon asked.

"None that I know of other than it's dry there too. What takes you to Canadian?"

"Buying a bull from Mr. Flemming," Turon answered.

"That'd be Colonel Flemming. Can be a tough man but a fair one. That's a nice gray. Can he run?" Pogue asked Levi.

"When he needs to." Levi thought of the race

through the rain.

"Está listo," Claudio called out.

The cowboys all rose from where they had been resting. Pogue urged his guests to the front of the line. Turon and Levi accepted and the grinning cook ladled beans, chile colorado, and set a generous stack of tortillas on their plates.

Claudio pointed to a platter of cakes. "Queque. How you say, pound cake?"

Both Turon and Levi balanced a sweet cake piece on their plates. Cups of coffee sat on a table that swung on hinges off the back of the wagon. Turon and Levi squatted and placed their coffee on the ground and began eating once Pogue joined them. Levi had never had food like this. He sipped coffee and watched the others tear their tortillas into quarters. Then folding the tortillas, one-handed into scoops where they could then push the food into the flat bread.

"Claudio, if you ever get tired of this outfit you may have to come to the Cherokee Nation," Turon said after trying the cake.

"Do not be stealing the cook," Pogue said. "Without him these boys couldn't afford the wages."

Claudio grinned widely and enjoyed the attention.

"You mentioned buying a bull. That sounds optimistic considering the talk going on about the Outlet closing." Pogue cocked his head to one side.

"Our outfit sold out. Wes Hatcher pulled stakes and went back to San Saba." Turon sipped his coffee.

"I helped Wes Hatcher years ago on a roundup. Good man to work for. So, you're buying a bull for another outfit?" Pogue asked.

"He's buying the bull." Levi pointed to Turon.

Pogue eyed Turon a little closer.

"Most cowboys can't save up enough to buy a horse, let alone a bull or cows." Pogue said, obviously impressed by Turon's ambition.

Most of the cowboys were young and on their first paying job. A few sized Turon up, trying to estimate what he was worth but knowing better than to ask.

Pogue continued. "I wish I had your ambition when I was younger. I thought about getting in on the run back in April in the unassigned lands. You would not believe how quick that country filled up. One morning where Guthrie Station is now, used to be prairie. By sundown, it was a tent city of ten thousand."

"Will it happen here?" Levi asked.

"No say, I don't know," Pogue said. "It's a different country. Good country for cattle when it rains. I can't see the plow ever making it here. Further east maybe."

Pogue studied Turon. "You may be smart."

"Few have accused me of that," said Turon.

"If the federals push the cattlemen out of this country the big outfits are over. These ranches won't survive." Pogue paused and used a finger to pick a piece of gristle from his teeth, then continued. "As long as the country needs beef, tallow, and hides, the little cowman may make it."

"I hope so," Turon said. "Little Kansas here wants to open a store. He will own a town one day. All I want is to raise cows."

Pogue stood and stretched. "Well, I hope you make it. The both of you. Might as well stay the night and get some of Claudio's biscuits in the morning. I need to ride out and tuck these heifers in. Unroll your beds anywhere you like," Pogue said with a wave of his hand.

Speaking in Spanish, Pogue divided up the night rider schedule then spoke in English to the Anglo cowboys. With that done he rode out to inspect the herd.

The next morning breakfast did not disappoint. Turon and Levi stood at the back of the line letting the

Day Brother's cowboys go first. When it was their turn Claudio made sure they had plenty of food. Even handed the two a flour sack full of biscuits and more of those pound cakes. The eastern horizon was beginning to glow as the sun rose.

Pogue shook hands with them both before climbing onto his horse.

"Buena suerte, you two. Safe travels," he said, looking down at them then turned to his men. "Ok boys, let's rattle some hocks."

Claudio waved from the wagon seat as he drove the team south. The familiar sound of cattle on the move filled the morning air. Turning their horses west and their backs on the departing herd, Turon wondered if they were turning their backs on something not long for this world.

CHAPTER 9

———♦«♦»♦———

Since leaving the Day Brothers' herd, Turon and Levi traveled on a well-worn wagon road. This was the California Road. Forty-two years of debris laid scattered along the wagon tracks. Horse and ox bones left to bleach in the sun. Occasionally one would see a broken axle, trash, or rotting canvas. Twenty thousand souls had crossed these plains in 1848 alone headed to the gold fields of California.

Turon and Levi watched the Antelope Hills on the western horizon. Rising above the surrounding plains they marked the boundary of what was the state of Texas as well as Cheyenne and Arapaho land.

In 1541 Coronado's Spaniards wrote about these hills. One hundred fifty years before the area would become the domain of the Comanche. One hundred and fifty years later a ragged band of Cheyenne and their Arapaho brothers held claim. Unknown to the tribes now in possession or the two cowboys who crossed it. The land would once again see a new group of people occupy it. This new group would plow, pump, and consume more from the land than all the people who ever came before.

"I've never been this far west," Levi said.

"Me neither. Texas is over there. Least part of it."

Turon raised his arm to point.

"What's Texas going to look like?"

"Like this, no more than we will see." Turon eyed an approaching wagon.

The two moved off the road and waited for the freight wagon to pass. The freighter talked to his mules as he came up even with Turon and Levi.

"Whoa there, whoa there." The driver pulled back on the leather reins of the six-up team of mules.

"Nice mules," Turon said.

"I aim to keep them."

"You can have them," replied Turon.

"You ain't Cheyenne or Arapaho. No beggar Indian. You've eaten too regular," the freighter said.

Turning to Levi, he asked. "Where you all bound to?"

"Colonel Flemming's place. Got business with him," Turon said before Levi could answer. He then jerked a thumb at Levi. "He does not speak English like us."

Levi sat in the saddle silent. He never knew what Turon was going to say at times like this, so he went along and watched for cues.

"He doesn't speak English?" The freighter asked.

"Nah, hardly speaks at all," Turon shook his head.

"What is he? Where is he from?"

"He is a Lilliputian," Turon said.

"A what?"

"Lilliputian. He is from the island nation of Lilliput over by Europe," Turon said straight-faced. "He does not say much but he works cheap. They are all little people. He is the tallest man from his country."

"Well, I swear. Seems like I heard of Lilliput," said the freighter.

"A whole shipload docked in New Orleans. I was down there delivering some horses to the army. Must have been four hundred of them wandering around looking for work. I picked him up and turned him into a cowboy."

The freighter shook his head and asked, "Why are they coming here?"

"Same as the rest of them immigrants. War and famine," Turon answered.

"The last thing we need is more people in this country. Not enough to go around as it is," the freighter grumbled.

Levi still sat silent.

"Can you tell us where the Flemming place is?" Turon asked sensing the freighter had enough of the conversation.

"You'll see a marker up the road a few miles. From there it's a day's ride to the colonel's place. Fourth drainage to the south, past the marker. Needmore Creek, they call it. Follow the wagon trail up the creek. You can't miss it."

"Why they call it Needmore Creek?" Turon asked.

"It's a nice creek; folks out there just need more of it." With that the freighter nodded and urged the mules forward talking to them and calling out their names.

"He must not have read *Gulliver's Travels*," Levi said as the wagon pulled out of earshot.

"I reckon not, Little Kansas. I would wager a bet that someone in Fort Reno has. Too bad we will not be there when he brings it up."

Raising a hand to the sun, Turon estimated how many hours they had left of daylight.

"We should be able to make another ten miles or so. One of those drainages will have a little water and place to camp maybe," he said as they urged their horses back on the trail.

They made the second drainage by nightfall and found enough water to make camp. Firewood was scarce and they gathered dried cow manure to use as fuel for a fire. Levi had learned to call them "cow chips."

The sky was clear, and the wind had calmed making the evening tolerable. Since crossing the Canadian River, they had experienced windy days. Wind rougher than on the eastern range of the Outlet.

"How far is it to your home?" Levi asked.

"Three hundred and twenty miles, I figure. Could be more depending on how we go," Turon said.

"One bull will be hard to drive."

"Yeah, been thinking about that. Easiest will be to break him to lead." Turon used a chip from the fire to light a cigarette.

"How long do you think it will take to get back to the Cherokee Nation?" Levi asked while staring up at the stars.

"Twenty-five, thirty days with a bull," Turon said while smoke trailed from his nostrils. "My tobacco is about gone. So is most of our food. We will need to provision in Canadian before we leave the country."

"I have money. I will pay my share," Levi said. "I only got two shells left for the shotgun."

"You can hunt a long time with two shells. Just cannot shoot much." Turon's expression was blank, but then a small grin formed. "We will go to the ranch first thing in the morning. If that freighter is right, we will be there before noon." Turon pitched the butt of the cigarette into the dwindling fire.

They had ridden for only an hour the next morning when they saw the first of the Flemming's Hereford cows. Twenty cows with calves walked in a line from the river where they had watered, the early morning sun illuminating them.

"Little Kansas, that is the prettiest sight I have ever seen."

Levi agreed. "The Hereford is quite an animal."

They continued to see little bunches of cattle scattered among the ravines along the river. Another hour went by, and a rider approached. Looked them both over hard before saying anything. He rode a small horse. Least the horse looked little compared to the rider's hat.

"Morning," the rider said in a nasally voice.

"Morning," Turon answered. "We are looking for the Flemming Ranch."

"You're on it," the rider said a bit sternly.

"Where can we find the colonel?" asked Turon.

"At the headquarters. But I will save you the trip. He ain't hiring."

"We're not looking for jobs," Turon said irritated.

"What you want with the colonel?" the rider asked.

"We are here to buy a bull."

"The Hell you say. Steal one more than likely," the rider said in a tone that even Levi took issue with as showed by his furrowed brow.

"Colonel Flemming is expecting us. I have a letter of introduction from Captain Wes Hatcher of San Saba, Texas. We are here on business." Turon pulled a folded paper from his saddle bag.

Turon started to hand the letter to the rider then pulled it back. "Or maybe you can't read."

"No need to get smart," the rider said. "We had problems with rustlers this year. To be honest, you do not look like bull buyers. Forgive me for my rudeness."

Turon nodded. "Forgive me for mine."

"Where are you fellows from?" asked the rider.

"Spring Creek over in the Cherokee Nation." Turon motioned with his hand to the east.

"I never been to that part of Texas," the rider commented. "Headquarters is up that next creek to the south. Cannot miss it," he said before riding away to the east.

As promised, one could not miss the headquarters of the Flemming Ranch. A large overhead entrance arched over the wagon road that paralleled the creek. Newly erected barbed wire fences held red- and white-faced cattle. One pasture had nothing but bulls in it.

A white house with a green roof sat at the center of the headquarters. A low structure that Turon assumed was a bunk house was halfway between the house and barns. A couple of men unloading rolls of barbed wire eyed them as they rode up.

"Howdy, where can we find the colonel?" Turon asked.

"He's at the house," one of them said and went back to the humiliating task of unloading the barbed wire. Only more humiliating for a free-range cowboy would have been building the fence.

"Much obliged," Turon said.

As they approached the house a man in his fifties stepped out onto the porch. Although he wore no uniform his stance and demeanor reflected years of military service. A low fence around the house protected flower beds that lined the front of the porch.

"Good day, gentlemen. How may I be of service?" greeted the colonel.

"Colonel Flemming?"

"Yes," nodded the colonel.

"My name is Turon Turtle. Mr. Hatcher suggested you may have a bull to sell."

"Ah, yes. I got his letter." The colonel looked at Levi.

"Levi Kuratowski," Levi said.

"Pole?" The colonel asked.

Levi nodded.

"I had a Pole serve with me during the war. Damn good soldier," the colonel said before continuing. "You men take your horses down to the first barn. You can turn them into the corral. There is a water trough, and you will find oats in the feed box." Indicating to the side of the house he continued, "Wash bowl is around that way. Dinner will be ready in a few minutes. We'll talk more then."

Someone rang a bell, and cowboys started converging on the house. Turon and Levi were last to use the wash bowl. They stood off to the side while the rest of the crew took their seats at a long table under the porch roof.

Colonel Flemming appeared in the doorway. "Mr. Turtle, Mr. Kuratowski, would you two join me inside?" The colonel turned back into the house.

The cowboys watched as Turon and Levi walked toward the door. Stepping inside they held their hats in front of them, letting their eyes adjust to the dim light. Levi felt uncomfortable. He thought they would be eating with the crew. Now they stood before a fine table with china plates and cups. If Turon felt uneasy he did not show it. Taxidermy elk and deer adorned the walls, and one massive buffalo head hung above a stone fireplace.

"Mr. Turtle, Mr. Kuratowski, it's an honor to have you in our home," a woman's voice said with a very British accent.

The attractive woman ushered them to the table and took their hats.

"Is it my understanding, Mr. Turtle that you are a Cherokee?" She peered directly into Turon's eyes.

For the first time Levi noticed Turon acting nervous.

"Yes, ma'am," he managed to say.

"How marvelous," she said with genuine glee.

"And you, sir? Mr. Kuratowski, is it?"

Levi nodded.

"Yes, ma'am." Levi managed to quote Turon.

"Poland," she said before continuing. "Imagine, us both so far from home. Meeting here of all places."

"Gentlemen, this is Mrs. Flemming, my wife." The colonel entered the room from the kitchen. Let's have a seat."

A plump woman appeared from the kitchen carrying a platter of fried beef steaks, roasted potatoes, and cornbread muffins that she set on the table before returning to the kitchen. Again, she appeared with a bowl of gravy and a pot of coffee. She poured coffee for the men before disappearing into the kitchen again only to return with a small pot of tea for Mrs. Flemming.

"Thank you, Martha. Martha is simply marvelous in the kitchen. She does the western dishes so well," Mrs. Flemming said.

As they ate, they talked of cattle, weather, and Turon's plans.

"The Hereford will work good for what you are wanting to do," Colonel Flemming said. "The Hereford will bring uniformity to your herd and the yearlings will outweigh your neighbors' at time of shipping. The heifers you keep will breed back sooner too. They are hardy animals."

Mrs. Flemming looked at her husband with conspiracy. "Yes, nothing more hardy than good British stock."

"I agree," Turon said while missing the innuendo. "Ever since I saw my first Hereford steers on the Outlet, I knew I wanted some for myself."

"We can ride through the bull pasture now if you would like," the colonel said.

"Is it far into town?" Levi asked changing the subject.

"Seven miles. There is a wagon trace from here that goes overland," the colonel said.

"Perhaps I can ride into town and pick up some supplies while you look over the bulls," Levi suggested.

Turon nodded.

"Owen, before you men ride off to do business, I simply must ask their thoughts on the origin theory." Mrs. Flemming used her husband's name rather than his title.

"They wouldn't be interested in that, my dear." The colonel was obviously embarrassed.

"Really? I beg to differ." Turning to Levi she continued. "Am I correct in assuming you are Jewish?"

"Yes, ma'am. I am." Levi looked unsure as he waited to see the point of the question.

"You see, Owen. When will I have an opportunity like this again?"

"Elizabeth. That theory is utter nonsense." The colonel looked all business but was not harsh.

Both Turon and Levi were unsure what to say but waited. Levi wishing to be on his way.

"Let us ask them," she said with an air of defiance about her. "Are either of you gentlemen familiar with the origin theory of the American Indian?"

"I cannot say I am," Turon said amused.

"No, ma'am," Levi simply said.

"You see, Mormonism has resurfaced an old theory, and it is getting attention," she spoke.

"Elizabeth," the colonel said in a pleading tone.

But she waved him off.

"There are scholars who believe that the Cherokee, for example, are the descendants of the lost tribe of Israel." She looked at Levi and spoke in a conspiratorial tone.

"I am not familiar with this," said Turon. "Is that just the Cherokee, ma'am, or all tribes?"

"All tribes of course," she answered.

Turon looked at Levi who had no response to such

a claim.

"Maybe the Cherokee. I'm not sure about the Muscogee or Osage." Turon thought it best to humor his host.

"You see, there is no mention of Indians in the Bible or Torah for that matter. All people must be accountable, or the ancient texts are wrong. The Bible is infallible; therefore, the only people missing are the lost tribe of Israel." Her eyes were intense as she made her point.

Levi continued to feel uncomfortable and wished to be on his way.

"Well, ma'am. You may have a point," Turon said.

She beamed. "Do go on," she said smiling.

"Most of the tribes have stories of first man and woman. Every tribe I know also has a story like Noah and the flood." Turon's voice was even.

"Are you hearing this, Owen?" she said excitedly. "Continue," she urged the visitors.

"Just maybe the Cherokee are not descendants of Jews, but the Jews are descendants of Cherokee."

Mrs. Flemming's expression was one of astonishment.

"The people of Arabia and Palestine are darker skinned. They do tend to be tribal." Her brow furrowed in thought.

"Our origin story is we came from an island. Maybe some of us sailed to Egypt. There are Pyramids here too," Turon said.

The colonel stood abruptly. "We better go look at some bulls. Excuse us, dear."

Levi and Turon both thanked Mrs. Flemming and retrieved their hats. Following the colonel out of the house they all headed to the barn where the horses were.

"She is a bit eccentric. I hope she did not offend you

two," the colonel apologized.

"Not at all. You cannot offend us with a meal like that," Turon said.

Saddling the horses the colonel offered a fresh mount for Levi so he could let the gray rest. Levi accepted the offer and rode west toward the town of Canadian with two canvas bags rolled up and tied behind the saddle. These he would use to carry the supplies back.

Turon and Colonel Flemming rode out toward the pastures. Turon was eager to see the Hereford stock.

Chapter 10

————◆«◆»◆————

The colonel wanted to show Turon some of the purebred cows as they crossed Needmore Creek. Passing through a gate Colonel Flemming could open from horseback, they rode into a pasture fenced with barbed wire.

"When we brought in the Herefords, we started using the fences to control what cows the bulls could breed. We still have range cattle that are half and three-quarter blood. You saw the wire the men were unloading. Fencing is the only way to control the breeding."

Turon nodded. "There's more and more going up all over."

"It's the future. Vital to operations like this. You cannot improve cattle on the open range unless everyone agrees on what bulls to use," Colonel Flemming said.

Raising his hand and pointing with his riding quirt he gestured to a group of cows in the shade of a rock outcrop. "These are part of the original fifty we brought from Illinois."

Turon surveyed the finest cattle he had ever seen and nearly became speechless. What cows were not in the shade of the outcrop stood in the open. Using their own bodies, they created shade for the calves that laid in their shadows.

"Notice how the cows make shade for their babies?" The colonel said with a hint of pride. "The heifers you keep will have those same motherly traits."

"You have fine cattle, Colonel," Turon finally managed to say.

"I wanted to show you these before we looked at the bulls."

"I saw some of your Herefords when we rode in this morning. They were good looking cattle. These are marvelous," Turon said stealing vocabulary from Mrs. Flemming.

"Those along the river were mostly half and three-quarter Herefords. The Hereford leaves its mark on the calves. Four generations from the original sire and you are likely to have a red with white-faced calf," the colonel said.

The bull pasture was mostly along the creek bottom. Yearling and two-year-old bulls lounged in the shaded high banks along the creek. A few older bulls held the deepest darkest portions of the shade.

"The old bulls are not for sale. Feel free to rouse any you want to see move," the colonel said.

"You have not mentioned a price." Turon knew he had to bring this up at some point.

"These are all full bloods. The two-year-olds are three hundred dollars. The yearlings are two hundred dollars. I have some three-quarter bloods cheaper, but I would not recommend those for what you want to do."

Turon studied the bulls. He rode through them in the easy manner of someone accustomed to cattle. Making one walk now and then to see how smooth they moved. To make the journey home the bull would need good feet. He would also need good feet to last on the limestone, flint ridges, and prairies of the Cherokee Nation.

On his second pass he singled out a bull with a great mass of white curly hair around his horns and forehead. As he moved and stepped out, the bull's muscles bunched and flexed under the deep red cherry hide. A white patch of hair called a feather neck ran down the top of his neck toward the shoulder. His tail involuntarily swatted and raked flies off the long back that gave way to high hip bones. Long legs moved smoothly and effortlessly across the ground.

"See one you like?" the colonel asked. "This one." Turon was firm in his decision.

"You have a good eye. I nearly kept him for myself." The colonel conveyed his approval of Turon's choice. "There's plenty of daylight left. We can drive him down to the trap by the barn where the oxen are. He can stay in there. I'll have a couple of men help you rope and throw him so you can brand him." The colonel rode closer to help Turon haze the bull from the rest of the herd.

Like most ranches, the Flemming Ranch had a forge for metal repairs. A man who was working it offered Turon the use of an iron rod. At home he would have had an actual branding iron.

"What's your brand look like?" asked the sweaty man working the forge.

Turon drew a circle in the dirt. At the top of the circle a mark stood for a head with a mark at the bottom showing a tail. Four more marks, two on either side of the circle, made the legs of a turtle.

"You're in luck," said the blacksmith.

He walked over to the barrel and pulled a branding iron from it with a forged circle. A couple of other irons were straight except for a two-inch elbow at the end. He thrust all into a pile of red coals in the middle of the forge.

"You two bring the bull to the back of the barn. Rope and stretch him out there." The blacksmith pointed to a doorway that opened to a pen next to the wire trap.

"Right or left side up?" one of the cowboys asked.

"Left. I will mark high on his hip," Turon said.

The two cowboys moved out and drove the bull and a few oxen into the pen. Turon closed the gate. The blacksmith walked out of the barn holding a red-hot circle brand and handed it to Turon.

In smooth efficiency one of the cowboys caught the horns of the bull. The bull lowered his head and pulled against the rope only to have the second cowboy catch his hind legs. Calmly with little fuss they stretched the bull from two different directions. The blacksmith did not hesitate to grab the bull's tail and pulled him to one side.

Turon moved swiftly and pushed the iron with even pressure to the bull's hide. Smoke flared from the singe of burnt hair. Removing the iron a plain circle appeared as leather shown. Running to the forge Turon grabbed the other two irons. Quickly he added the marks needed to complete his brand. From a tin can the blacksmith used a well-worn brush and lathered a dark substance onto the fresh brand.

"Pine tar, keep the flys from blowing the scar." The blacksmith moved and placed a knee on the neck of the bull. Turon instantly removed the rope from around the horns. Turon and the blacksmith stepped back, and the bull kicked free from the heel rope. Annoyed, but not upset, the bull walked over to the oxen and butted one out of his way.

The cowboys gathered their ropes and rode through the barn avoiding gates. The blacksmith plunged the irons into a bucket of water to cool them.

Closing the gate to the pen Turon watched the bull. He thanked the blacksmith and walked to the house where Colonel Flemming was preparing a bill of sale.

Mrs. Flemming congratulated Turon and escorted him to an office off the dining room where the colonel motioned him to sit.

"It's customary to give a name to a seed-stock bull. Especially if you intend to sell bulls from him later. Any name you would like to put on the papers?"

"Bushyhead," Turon said.

The colonel asked no questions and filled the name out on the papers. Turon pulled a leather wallet from his waistband. It held two year's worth of wages and everything he had withdrawn from the Bank of Caldwell before he left on this trip. He counted and placed three hundred dollars on the desk and stuffed the wallet back into place. Colonel Flemming handed him the bill of sale and papers. Setting the money aside without counting it he reached and shook Turon's hand.

"When do you plan to leave, Mr. Turtle?" the colonel asked.

"In the morning if possible. I have been away from home for a good while."

"I can understand that. You and Mr. Kuratowski will stay in the spare room tonight. You can head out after breakfast," the colonel said.

"You have treated us well, Colonel. I did not know what to expect when I came here."

"You are a cowman. You appreciate good stock. A philosopher as well. Mrs. Flemming will have new ammunition to use after your talk earlier. In a few years, you'll want another bull. Maybe a few cows. I'll be here when you do."

"I hope to come back," Turon said.

"Do not just hope, make it happen. You are a young

man. Times are changing but those who can read the signs can get out ahead of the change. You took a risk coming here. You paid a lot of money for this bull." The colonel paused before speaking again. "Are you married Mr. Turtle?"

"No. I am not."

"Find a woman. A woman of valor. Raise cattle and children. Then see me for more bulls."

Turon respected this man. He was certainly a cattleman and would pay close attention to his thoughts on cattle. The finding a woman part though, he wasn't sure about. He did not see a future in that.

"I will keep it in mind, Colonel. The buying more bulls at least. Women are a mystery to me."

"They are a mystery to every man. I understand cattle, I can read a battlefield. I can make sense of God's will. However, no number of books, education, or personal experience can prepare you to understand a woman." The colonel's face broke into a grin.

The colonel had some work to do in the late afternoon. Turon excused himself and walked down to the wire trap where the bull was keeping a respectable distance from the oxen.

It was there Levi found Turon lost in thought watching the bull.

"That him?" Levi said, startling Turon.

"Yeah, that is him."

"Nice bull, as good as I've ever seen." Levi said approvingly.

"How did you make out in town?" Turon looked at the sacks stuffed with goods.

Levi turned to see if anyone was close enough to hear him.

"I posted a letter with fifty dollars to the marshal in Caldwell," Levi said above a whisper.

"Whose name did you sign?" Turon asked.

"Lemuel Gulliver." Levi once again spoke just above a whisper.

Turon shook his head and smiled.

"Now just to be safe, you should trade that horse off once we are back in the Nations," Turon suggested.

Nodding, Levi agreed. "He is the best horse I have ever ridden."

"I know. Even with that brand though, you could be recognized if we ever came across that marshal," Turon said.

The good feeling he had after posting the money was disappearing. Turon could see it in his expression.

"We've been invited to supper and to stay the night in the house," Turon said.

"In the house?" asked Levi in disbelief.

"Yup, feather bed and all."

Someone rang a bell for supper, and cowboys once again converged on the house. Turon moved to lift the canvas sacks from the horse.

"We better stow these supplies and rub this horse down before turning him out. Then get some vittles." Turon said stepping to the canvas sacks.

The cowboys were once again at the long table on the porch. They eyed the full-blooded Cherokee and short stranger as they came into the house. Mrs. Flemming once again took their hats. Once again, she questioned Turon and Levi on their respected cultures, while the colonel politely objected shifting the conversation to the state of the cattle industry and regional politics.

CHAPTER 11

————◆‹‹◆››◆————

Breakfast came early. Orange light streaked across the eastern horizon as Turon and Levi saddled their horses. The pinto stood with pack filled and Turon took a length of rope. He left it easily accessible on the pack.

"What's the rope for?" asked Levi.

"That bull will be easy enough to drive for a few miles. Once he decides he has had enough he will try to turn back. That is when he will learn the rope."

The blacksmith came over and joined the conversation. "He'll lead like a milk cow after a few days."

"How much do we owe you for horseshoes?" Turon realized the blacksmith had taken it upon himself to check the feet of their horses.

"The colonel pays me. He says tend to your horses, that's what I do."

"Much obliged at any rate," Turon said.

Levi opened the gate to the trap so Turon could ride in and sort the bull from the oxen. The bull moved as Turon slowly hazed him through the gate and barn lot. Finding new grass, the bull stopped to eat. Colonel Flemming walked up to the barn where Levi was closing the gate. He shook Levi's hand and wished him luck. Stepping over to Turon he reached up and shook hands with the young Cherokee.

"You are a cattleman now. I expect to hear from you in a few years when you need another bloodline."

"Thank you, Colonel. Appreciate it," Turon said. Then to Levi, "Let's go, Little Kansas."

Turon hazed the bull down the wagon road. Levi led the pinto so Turon could maneuver in case the bull turned back or broke into a run in the wrong direction. They had managed three miles before the bull tried to turn back. He had smelled a small herd of cows and wanted to investigate.

Turon rode up by the pinto and snatched the extra rope from the pack. The bull grazed so Turon had Levi stop. Still sitting in the saddle Turon took the rope in his hands. He tied a small eye loop in the rope leaving eighteen inches or so of tail. Fishing the long tail of the rope through the eye he then took the short piece and tied a knot allowing the rope to move freely. This created a large loop that would be the headstall and a smaller loop that would go around the bull's muzzle and chin. Once on the bull's head it would not constrict the airway of the bull allowing Turon to control where the bull traveled.

Riding close to the bull Turon made a short toss and the headstall landed neatly around and behind the bull's horns. The bull raised his head at this new accessory. In doing so the slack chin loop flopped down below the bull's muzzle. At this moment Turon jerked the slack snugging the rope halter in place.

Shaking his head and tugging on the rope the bull tested this new annoyance. Turon slipped the loop he had tied on the other end over the saddle horn. Letting the bull take up the slack the rope tightened turning the bull to face Turon.

"If he charges, take your rope and double hock

him," Turon said as Levi shook out a loop from his own rope and dropped the lead line to the pinto who looked on at this show with indifference.

The bull stood still for a long moment keeping tension on the rope halter. Deciding to turn and try making a run he flicked his tail and lowered his head. Turon anticipated this and had the bay turned and pulled the bull into the bay's direction before the bull could get momentum. After several attempts to run with no success the bull stood still. Patiently Turon waited. The bull went back to grazing occasionally shaking his head. Turon tugged on the rope and the bull stepped toward the rider and horse on the other end. Soon Turon led the way with the bull following with minimal objection. Levi urged the gray to follow leading the pinto. It was in this order they traveled down the California Road toward home.

They pushed the bull hard the first day, reasoning a tired bull would not try to make a run to his home range. By the time the sun was setting, the Antelope Hills were ablaze in the retreating light and the bull had surrendered to the rope. They made camp and again used cow chips for fuel.

"I nearly forgot," Levi said jumping to his feet to rummage through a canvas sack. From the sack he produced a leather strap with a buckle at one end. Digging further he retrieved a cow bell.

"I figure we could use it to keep track of the bull. In case he got away we could follow the sound." Levi held the bell and strap out to Turon.

"That is a good idea, Little Kansas. I should have thought of that." Turon stood to look the bell over.

He then reached into a sack of cornbread muffins the Flemming's cook had given them after breakfast that morning.

The bull was lying down staked out near the horses

but turned his head to watch Turon approach. Turon spoke softly as he reached for the rope with one hand while presenting a corn muffin to the bull with his other. The bull hesitated then ate the muffin from Turon's hand. Turon slipped the leather strap around the bull's neck buckling it where it hung loose. Handing the bull another muffin Turon spoke softly and walked away. The bull did not seem to mind the strap or bell.

"He is worn out. We will take it easy tomorrow. Let him graze. I doubt he tries to run again. He is halter broke," Turon said returning to Levi and the fire.

"Have you decided on what way we will go?" asked Levi.

"I have been thinking about that. The most traveled and easiest would be to stay on this trace to the old Texas Road. Then up through the Creek Nation to home." Turon said while squatting on his heels.

"That's a lot of farmsteads, milk cows, and yard dogs to get by," Levi said thinking of moving the bull through the settlements.

"Yeah, he has never been to town. Wouldn't want him to pick up rude habits. There is another way I am thinking." Turon said. "We could go further down river. Cut northeast avoiding Fort Reno. Might be dry but it's not a far stretch to the North Canadian and on to the Cimarron River. Then down the Cimarron to the Arkansas all the way to Tulsey Town. From there east we should find plenty of water and grass."

Levi looked off to the northeast. "Might be more grass that way. The grass is scarce along this road."

"We will have to cross the new boomer settlements by Guthrie. They have only been there since April. May be more grass that way than the southern route." Turon laid a new cow chip on the fire.

"Could be." Levi sat nodding. "By the way, what do you think about Mrs. Flemming believing the Cherokee are a lost tribe of Israel?"

Turon chuckled. "I do not know. The world is old. Older than we know, Little Kansas. Jesus was a Jew, was he not?"

Nodding, Levi acknowledged the question. "Yes, he was a Jew. According to your Bible," Levi said respectfully.

"Then there you have it," Turon said.

"There I have what?" Levi asked in confusion.

"Jesus," Turon said. "Everyone knows that Jesus was a quarter Cherokee. On his mother's side." Turon then rolled into his blanket flipping the canvas flap of the bedroll over him.

From under the blanket and canvas he wished Levi a goodnight and sought sleep. Levi soon did the same.

Chapter 12

————◆«◆»◆————

Although the days were still warm in the fading summer, the nights were cooler. Antelope were beginning to rut and the bucks fought over does in heat. The third morning Turon took the opportunity to shoot an antelope buck that had come within range of his Henry rifle.

Fortunate for them he did so. Returning to camp with the antelope slung over the back of the pinto he carried his rifle across the saddle resting in his hand. Levi had stayed to keep an eye on the bull and watch camp.

Turon heard the voices before he came over a slight rise and saw the four Cheyenne outnumbering Levi. One of the Cheyenne had the bull's lead rope in his hands and the short Levi held a shotgun pointed in the man's direction.

The Cheyenne wore humorous expressions and were all taunting the little Jewish cowboy. Their faces changed however as Turon rode in now holding the rifle one handed up in the air. It was ready to come down in any direction he chose.

"What is going on here?" Turon asked.

"They say they are going to eat the bull." Levi was

relieved to have Turon back.

The Cheyenne looked over the full-blooded Cherokee Turon and spoke Cheyenne, but Turon could not understand.

Turon spoke rapid Cherokee in an authoritative voice. The Cheyenne looked at one another never hearing Cherokee spoken. Finally, the oldest of the four spoke in English.

"We are hungry. You have meat." He pointed at the bull.

"No, the bull is not for meat. He is for cows," Turon said sternly.

"You cross our land, you must pay." The Cheyenne pointed at Turon, then pointed back to the bull.

Turon hated to give up the antelope, but it might be necessary to keep the bull. So, he pulled the pinto forward and pulled the slip knot that held the antelope. It fell to the ground and the pinto stepped away from the carcass that had been on his back.

"Take the meat. Leave the bull alone." Turon pointed at the antelope on the ground.

Turon and the older Cheyenne stared at each other, with neither saying a word. The silence spoke volumes that this was Turon's only and final offer.

"Good. We take meat. You leave or we take the bull," the older Cheyenne said before peppering the Cheyenne holding the rope with commands unfamiliar to the cowboys.

The Cheyenne who had been threatening to take the bull released the rope and grabbed the antelope hoisting it on a shoulder. Another Cheyenne took it and draped it over his horse's back.

Turon and Levi watched the four riders leave laughing.

"Little Kansas, the Indian fighter," Turon said.

"They were going to take him." Levi still watched

the Cheyenne ride away.

"They might have. Never know what them Indians will do," Turon said with a smile. "We should take turns sleeping for a few nights. Least till we get off this reservation."

They crossed the river to where the grass was better. Taking their time. Making sure to let the bull graze so he would not lose body condition. The bull grew accustomed to the routine. The slightest tug of the rope and he would follow. Levi continually scanned the horizon watching for any sign of riders.

"See any Indians?" Turon asked on one occasion.

"Just one," Levi joked.

When they came to the North Canadian, they found water and did not have to use the shovel. Turkeys were abundant and walnut trees grew along the river bottom among cottonwoods and cedars. They followed the river to where it turned southeast toward Fort Reno. Then continued east across the open prairie. Topping a rise, they saw a thin line of trees run along a stream. From the hill they could see that the creek flowed north and turned northeast.

"We should be able to follow this drainage all the way to the Cimarron," Turon said.

Levi nodded. Then catching movement down below the hill near the creek he pointed. Turon turned and looked.

Horses trotted out of the timber. Three mares and two had colts following them plus a yearling. They watched as the horses grazed, and the colts ran circles chasing each other.

"I think they are mustangs or at least they are now," Turon said.

"Maybe they got away from a cow outfit?" Levi wondered aloud.

"Or Indian ponies," Turon replied.

"I don't see a stallion." Levi scanned the surrounding area.

"If there is one, he will be around somewhere close."

"If so, he won't like us stealing his mares," Levi said.

"We got the rope and time. If they wear brands, we will leave them be. If not, we will brand them and take them with us," Turon said as he watched the horses.

"I would not want to take someone's horses," Levi said flatly.

"Strange talk for a horse thief, Little Kansas." Turon chuckled. "Being this far out, I would say they are wild. If they ain't branded, they are fair game."

"If it is legal and the custom, then all right." Levi agreed.

"Let us ease down toward the trees. We will stake out the pinto and bull. Then get a closer look." Turon moved down the slope.

Staying downwind of the horses, they found a good place to camp. Levi stripped the pack off the pinto and tied his lead rope to a cottonwood limb. Turon did the same with the bull leaving him enough slack to reach the grass that grew in the creek bottom.

They pulled some extra rope from the pack and Turon tied a honda knot in a couple of ropes and built some loops.

"You have the fastest horse. Pick out one of the mares with a colt. Rope her and hold her. I will come in and slip a rope on her head like we did the bull. Only I will tie a hind leg up with the slack or tie her to a tree limb if one is at hand. She should not go anywhere." Turon made sure Levi knew the plan.

Levi did not grow up in the west but in his couple of years on the plains he had become proficient with the rope and groundwork. He had learned to use leverage when throwing a calf or yearling. Sore muscles turned him into an excellent rider as he learned to move with the horse, not against it.

"We've never roped anything off the gray." Levi's face showed concern.

"He will be okay. If he breaks into two let go of the mare and stay on," Turon said.

They rode and got closer to the little group of horses than they expected. They watched them and Turon looked over the shoulders and hips. None of the horses had brands, and their manes were long.

Turon pointed at a line-backed dun mare. "See if you can catch her," he said in a muffled voice.

Levi nodded and shook out a loop. The gray's ears pointed forward as he eyed the horses. Levi urged the gray to step out and rode toward the mares in a way that put him between them and the timber along the creek. The mares nickered as he moved closer. The dun started to walk toward the trees and broke into a trot as Levi spurred the gray to cut her off.

The gray understood the task and soon Levi was in position and sailed a loop over the mare's head. Jerking the slack tight around her neck, the mare spun and reared. Turon was quick and was at once in position with the bay and slipped the rope halter over the mare's nose and pulled the headstall tight.

"Hold her!" He shouted and tossed the tail of the rope over a cottonwood limb. Forming a quick slipknot, Turon tugged on it making it secure.

Levi gave the rope slack as Turon rode back up to the side of the dun mare. Hooking two fingers under the loop that was around the dun's neck he pulled the slack making the loop large enough the mare was able to run through it.

Sensing a freedom from the neck rope the mare made a quick run for escape. The rope halter tied to the limb tightened around her head. The limb bent against her weight as she took up the slack. The mare bent the limb only to have the stored tension of it pull her back.

Levi coiled his rope looking around. The other horses had not gone far and Turon signaled toward another mare, a strawberry roan, who was sniffing out her colt. Building a loop Levi urged the gray forward. Confused as to why its mother did not run away, the dun's colt ran to her. This caused the other colt to follow its young herd mate. The second colt's mother nickered and ran after it making Levi's throw a success.

Again, Turon had the bay close in and pitched the other rope halter over the mare's nose jerking the headstall behind her ears. With a flick of his wrist the halter pulled tight. The mare turned away and tried to kick the bay, but Turon spun the bay away avoiding the roan's hind feet.

"Take her to the cedar!" Turon shouted.

Staying on either side of the mare as she reared and lunged one way then the other, they led her close to a cedar tree that stood at least ten feet tall. Turon rode the bay close to the tree and flipped the rope over and around the top part. Doing this twice he made the rope fast and wheeled the bay out of harm's way as the roan lunged at him.

"Let her go!" he shouted.

Riding off a little way they watched each mare fight their tree. The strawberry roan doubled the cedar one way then the other, but its roots held. The dun soon stopped fighting the limb and stood keeping tension on the rope.

The mare and yearling they had not roped stood off some distance away, too far to chase but close enough to keep an eye on. The colts of the captured mares went to their mothers unsure what had just happened.

"That worked," Turon said.

"What do we do now?" Levi asked.

"We wait. They will learn the rope like the bull did. Tomorrow, we will take them to water," Turon said. "Might as well make camp."

Two days they stayed along the creek. With ample wood and water, it was an ideal spot. The bull grazed and laid in the shade. The pinto stayed close to the bull as the animals had become accustomed to one another.

Once as Levi had ridden out in search of quail, he glimpsed the mare and yearling that had gotten away. Following them he soon saw another group of horses. Upon seeing Levi and the gray, a brown-colored stallion ran back and forth along the small herd urging his mob into a run. They traveled west and Levi followed. Satisfied they were leaving the area he turned back toward camp. Soon he found a covey of quail where he spent five shells and took five birds.

Both Turon and Levi worked with the captured mares. The mares learned quickly and were agreeable to being led to water. They moved the mares to new areas, so they had grass. The colts never got far and were getting accustomed to Turon and Levi.

"Which mare do you want?" Turon asked Levi while waiting on coffee to boil.

"I don't know, it was your idea," Levi said.

"I'm partial to the dun mare, but both are good framed." Turon squatted by the fire.

"I'll take the roan if you don't mind then." Levi added, "What do we do with them?"

"Break to ride and keep them or sell them once we come to a settlement. They both are smart. They took to the rope quick." Turon poured two cups of coffee.

"Those colts are stout looking," Levi said accepting the coffee.

"Yeah, we did all right on this deal so far. Just have to make it home." Turon blew steam from his cup.

The two days working with the mares gave their stock plenty of rest and a chance to fill up on grass. On the third morning they rode east to another drainage Turon had noticed while scouting the area. It too ran north and east, and they decided it might be a shorter way to get to the Cimarron River.

Turon led the way with the bull following close behind. Behind the bull Levi rode the gray leading the pinto with his pack. Tied to the pinto the dun mare followed obeying the rope. The strawberry roan's halter rope was spliced into the dun's tail. She too obeyed the rope, and the colts trotted alongside their mothers when they were not darting between animals and riders, to the annoyance of the pinto and bull. On the strawberry roan's forearm, the number forty was freshly branded, and the dun carried the Turtle mark as did the colts whose brands matched their mothers.

For half the day they rode following the drainage Turon had found. They could see from a ridge the creek ran into a canyon. A canyon that held springs based on the trees they had seen below. Old buffalo trails crisscrossed the ridge, but all seemed to go into the canyon.

"It will take us a while to get down there but should be a good place to camp." Turon pointed out the canyon.

"I could live here." Levi nodded.

"Not sure your store would have many customers way out here," Turon said while urging the bay forward.

"If I fail with the store, I will come here and catch horses." Levi pulled the pinto's lead rope as the gray stepped out to follow the bull and bay.

The trail down into the canyon was well worn. Buffalo, followed by man on horses made trails that had been used for centuries. Once in the canyon a meadow opened before them. Large walnut trees grew competing for sunlight against the red rock outcrops. A slight breeze blew through the leaves and green balls of the walnut fruit clung to their limbs, occasionally releasing, and plummeting to the canyon floor.

"Looks like buzzards." Levi pointed above the tree line.

"They are buzzards," Turon said as he watched the circling birds.

The bull suddenly showed great interest in his surroundings. He lifted his head smelling the air.

"What's wrong with the bull?" Levi asked.

"Acts like he smells cows," Turon said, and as if on cue the bull bawled his long cry announcing his presence. The sound echoed throughout the canyon.

A brindle cow with sharp upright horns appeared from the brush. She had a halter on her head and was dragging a length of rope. The bull moved up even with Turon and the bay. He continued his bawling at the cow.

"Someone's milk cow it looks like." Turon pointed at the udder and swelled teats.

Turon dropped the bull's lead line and let him investigate the cow.

"That cow's in heat," Levi said telling the obvious.

"What is a milk cow doing out here? Who does she belong to?" Turon asked even knowing Levi would not have an answer.

"She's mine," a woman's voice said in a tone proving ownership.

Turon turned and where the cow had materialized out of the brush, a woman now stood. A young woman. She stood tall, with her shoulder's back. She wore no bonnet, and her black hair pulled back in one braid. A blue threadbare sun-faded dress moved in the breeze. A double barrel shotgun laid cradled in her arm. Her free hand rested on the comb of the stock. Ready if needed. Her dark eyes peered over high cheeks. Her expression evidence she would tolerate no foolishness. Turon had a vision, clarity of thought. This was the most beautiful woman he had ever seen. And she would be his wife.

CHAPTER 13

———◆"◆"◆———

Lorelei Dixon stood at the edge of the brush looking at the strangers. Cowboys, she thought, based on their attire. One sat on a gray horse and led a string of horses, one of the horses carried a pack. The cowboy who turned the bull loose sat in the saddle staring at her. His dark eyes stared out past a face free of whiskers although he was very much a man. Broad shoulders gave way to sinewy arms. Rough hands accustomed to labor matched the copper-toned face. Indian she thought, what tribe she had no idea.

Levi waited for the usually talkative Turon to say something, but he seemed transfixed not saying a word. Just sat there staring at the woman or girl. Levi was no judge of weights or age in either women or livestock. This one looked to be seventeen or eighteen.

Finally, Levi spoke breaking the silence. "Good afternoon, ma'am. We did not expect to find a farm this far out."

"You are apt not to either. We have a camp down at the spring," she said shifting her eyes from Turon to Levi then back to Turon.

"I am Turon Turtle. This is Levi Kuratowski. Most people call him Little Kansas. That is Bushyhead mingling with your cow," Turon finally said while pointing at the bull.

"I am Lorelei Dixon. You did not introduce your horses," she said with a faint smile.

"I make it a habit not to name an animal I may have to eat." Turon was stoned-faced.

The two stared at each other long enough to make Levi feel uncomfortable. The bull smelled the cow's tail area, raising his head, and curled his upper lip. It was Levi who spoke again not accustomed to taking charge of a conversation.

"Your cow may not be in a mood to stand for milk." Levi broke the silence again.

As if she noticed the cow for the first time, she spoke.

"I can turn the calf out on her. We have plenty of milk anyhow. Would you gentlemen care to come to camp? It will be time to start supper soon," she offered.

Turon turned the bay and rode to the cow's lead rope. In one motion he leaned from the saddle effortlessly catching up the tail of the rope. Taking a dally around the saddle horn he turned the bay to face Lorelei.

"Lead the way." Turon pushed the bay forward. "Would you care to ride?" He offered his own horse.

"It's not far." She turned and walked down one of the many old buffalo trails.

They only traveled a little way through a thicket of oak and cedar to a clearing. An old Studebaker army wagon was parked on the far side of the clearing. A canvas tarp strapped and tied to the bows provided shelter from sun and rain. A mule grazed out in the clearing, and a calf bawled in the distance as the cow came into its line of sight.

Turon took in the camp with the grass grazed down in patches where the mule previously had been staked.

A good-sized stack of firewood was nearby. Not far the buzzards circled north of the clearing on the far side of the canyon.

"Something die?" Turon asked Lorelei.

"Our Jenny mule. We dragged her over there." She motioned toward the area below the circling buzzards.

"What happened to her?" Turon asked.

As if from the heavens a deep booming voice spoke.

"Colic, if you believe that. I always heard a mule would not colic, but this one did." A tall man stepped from behind the wagon, leaned a rifle against the rear wheel, and came forward. "Dan Conner. Who are your friends, Lorelei?"

Turon and Levi introduced themselves.

"There's a fine spring down there." He pointed a finger toward the canyon's edge. "There's plenty of room to stake your stock out in the clearing. Girl, there is a turkey hanging on a limb back there. Fetch it for supper," the tall Dan commanded.

Setting her shotgun down beside the rifle she moved quick to the rear of the wagon to clean the turkey. Turon and Levi saw to it the horses and bull had an opportunity to drink and staked them out all except the bull. With the bulling cow it would be impossible to keep him away from her, so Turon turned him loose after seeing Mr. Conner tie the cow to an oak sprout and letting her calf attack the swollen teats with fury.

It was customary for farm families to split the cow's milk with the calf. Often it was two teats for the family and two for the calf. That way they were able to raise a heifer to one day milk, or a steer to one day eat or sell. The part of the milk for the family went to make butter, cheese, cook with, or drink. A good milk cow was vital to a family's survival on the frontier.

The deep booming voice announced to Turon and Levi they were free to unload their gear at their camp site and stay for supper.

"We have coffee we can offer." Levi pulled a tin from the packsaddle.

"I will accept. We have been rationing ours," Dan said.

"How long you been here?" Turon asked sitting his saddle down opposite where the tall man squatted.

"Six weeks here, before that Lisbon. They call it Kingfisher now. Before that, Guthrie." He glanced off to the side for a moment. "We left Alma, Arkansas in March. Made it in time for the run by April twenty-second." He paused while Turon and Levi waited to hear more. "I made the run and staked my claim on Ephraim Creek, only to arrive at the land office to find someone had already filed on it. When I returned to visit with the man who had claimed it, he had friends. Armed friends," he said.

"The law couldn't do anything?" Levi asked.

"What law?" Lorelei said as she walked around the wagon carrying the turkey carcass.

"There were a lot of claims," Dan said. "Some were double-filed or outright stolen. We moved into a camp near Guthrie and waited until June to have our hearing. The other man had better witnesses. The right friends. From there we moved to Lisbon to another camp. Could not find a claim or afford a town lot. Maisie took the cough." He paused again for a long moment.

Turon watched Lorelei move around the camp kitchen area. Coals smoldered and soon the cooking fire was going as she lowered a cast iron oven into a shallow pit. She occasionally glanced his way.

"Maisie was my wife, Lorelei's mother. We buried her south of King Fisher's Stage Station." The man was silent for a little while.

"I'm sorry to hear that," Levi finally said.

"It was a shame. We sold two of the mules to buy supplies. That whole territory has gone mad. We thought we would strike west for New Mexico or Colorado. Made it this far before the mule got sick." He looked at Lorelei. "Might just stay here," he added.

"Sooner or later the Cheyenne will show up on a hunt. They will not hurt you. Might try to eat your mule or cow. They will for sure send for the soldiers. They will say you are squatting on their land," Turon said with sincere concern.

"Them soldiers are more than welcome to haul us out of here," Dan said. "Not to change the subject, but how did you get a bull like that?" Dan waved a hand toward the Hereford bull.

Turon explained how he had saved up money. That he and Levi had worked for the same outfit and rode out to the Texas Panhandle to pick out the bull and were now taking it back to the Cherokee Nation.

"Cherokee, you say. Hear that, Lorelei? He's Cherokee, too," Dan said while Lorelei moved around preparing a meal. "Her mother was part Cherokee they say. I am not her blood father you see. Her mother had been married before, but her father drowned in the Arkansas when the Glory May's boiler blew up below Little Rock."

Turon nodded. He had heard of Cherokee, especially the old settlers, who had married whites and stayed in Arkansas after removals.

Lorelei continued to prepare food but kept watching Turon. He watched her move about with grace and swiftness. Dan kept an eye on them both.

"Are you a cattleman too, Little Kansas?" Dan asked.

"No, I don't own any cows like Turon. I do have a plan to buy a wagon and trade in the Cherokee Nation. Maybe open a store one day," Levi said.

"Hear that, Lorelei? We have two empire builders here for supper." Dan eyed both Turon and Levi. "That's a nice horse you're riding there. The gray looks like he could travel well. Run too if I were guessing." Dan said while appraising the gray.

Throughout the meal they visited. The turkey was well prepared, and Lorelei had made biscuits. The time in the canyon had given them opportunity to make butter from the milk cow, which they all lathered onto the biscuits along with honey that came from a nearby bee tree.

Dan Conner was a real talker. He told stories about the Arkansas River valley. Wild stories of river men, outlaws, and feuding landowners. Turon matched wits the best he could but Levi noticed he was distracted.

It occurred to Levi that Turon was acting like the bull Bushyhead. He rarely took his gaze from Lorelei. If he did it was only for a moment, then he would watch her again as she cleaned up or fetched tobacco for Dan's pipe, who in turn shared it with Turon so he could roll a cigarette.

Levi enjoyed the visit, and the food was superior to anything they had had since leaving the Flemming's ranch. However, he was ready to get back on the trail. The days spent breaking the mustangs to lead worried him. There was nothing to be gained staying in this canyon any longer than what would be necessary. Breakfast and farewells then off to the Cimarron.

Dan turned to Levi asking about Poland and coming to America.

"I better check on the stock. You visit, Little Kansas. I have nearly worn myself out keeping you entertained." Turon stood and stretched before walking into the growing darkness of the canyon.

Turon walked down to where the horses were

picketed. The colts were close to their mothers and the pinto stood off to the side showing indifference to the whole outfit. The bull lay close to the cow and calf. Checking the knots on all the horses and the mule, Turon decided to get a drink from the spring. Kneeling he cupped water and brought it to his lips.

"The horses all right?" Lorelei walking up carrying a bucket to the spring.

"Yes ma'am, all tucked in." Turon took the bucket from her and dipped it into the clear pool.

They both stood for a moment staring at each other until Lorelei spoke.

"Tell me about where you're from," she said.

"What do you want to know?" Turon set the bucket down on a flat rock.

"What's it like?" she asked.

"It is a green country. Open prairies mixed with hardwood timber and tall pines on the hills and ridges. Some bottomlands that will grow anything you want to plant," he said.

"Sounds nice. Do you have a family?" she asked.

"I do. My mother and father have a farm. I have a sister and little brother. He's twelve and she's eighteen."

"How old are you?" she asked.

"Twenty-one in about a month. How old are you?"

"Eighteen," she said thinking in her mind that eighteen and twenty-one was not that big of a difference. "Are you married?"

"No," Turon said then asked, "Are you?"

A burst of soft laughter erupted from her.

"No." She smiled and shook her head.

They talked. And laughed. The bucket of water slowly leaked out as it had served its purpose as an excuse for her to come to the spring. As they talked neither paid any attention to the full moon on the eastern horizon. Large and drenched in orange light, it rose, finally illuminating the canyon floor.

Levi glanced occasionally toward the spring where he could see two figures sitting on a rock.

What could they have to talk about?

Dan also watched the two talking and a thought took root in his mind; one he kept to himself.

As the couple by the spring continued to talk, Dan continued to quiz Levi. Dan was an avid reader when books were at hand. He found it interesting that Levi had learned English not only from working with the cowboys but through reading books.

"*Gulliver's Travels* is an old one but a good one," Dan said.

Levi nodded. "It's my favorite. But I have a new book. It's good too. A woman wrote it."

"A woman? What's her name?" Dan asked.

"Jules Vern."

Dan roared with laughter. "Jules Vern is a man. A Frenchman, but a man nonetheless."

Dan stood and walked to the wagon, then came back with a book and handed it to Levi.

"Have you read this one?"

Levi held it in the moonlight, and could make out the title, *Kidnapped* by Robert Louis Stevenson.

"No, I haven't." Levi's face showed excitement to be holding an unfamiliar book in his hands.

"Take it. I've read it ten times."

"Thank you. I can pay you," Levi said.

"Don't insult me." Dan waved off the offer.

They talked of books, far off countries, and the changing times. The moon was high above illuminating the canyon floor. Turon and Lorelei still sat on the rock near the spring. The campfire burned low, and Dan placed some nearby sticks on it and flames flared up. Levi dropped his head slightly and jerked it up.

"You might as well get some sleep, Little Kansas." Dan said in a soft but deep voice. "Don't worry, I'll chaperone from here."

Levi glanced toward the spring at the two figures in the moonlight.

"What could they be talking about?" His voice sounded sleepy, and he soon nodded off.

Turon looked into her eyes as she spoke. He could see the moon reflected in her eyes. He knew it was late, and he knew her stepfather watched from a distance. The fact he did not call her away or intervene put Turon at some ease.

"I am of the Bird Clan of the Cherokee," he told her, expecting her to understand.

"I don't know what clan my mother belonged to. I guess I really know little of my mother's family."

"If you do not know your clan, then you are not Cherokee," he said quietly.

"Does that matter?" she asked.

Turon was quiet for only a moment.

"No. It does not." He reached for her. His hands, rough with calluses and rope burn scars, held Lorelei's hands. Her hands too showed signs of hard labor. Holding each other's hands they each experienced a surge of excitement. Enhanced by the light of the moon and cool air the surge compelled them to embrace. Turon kissed the lips of the woman he would marry. Lorelei clung tight to the man she knew held her future.

A knowing Dan watched the two figures in the moonlight merge into one. They soon stood and walked toward the campfire. Only releasing each other's grip when they came to the outer reaches of the fire light. Turon laid down near the snoring Levi commenting that he did not realize how late it was.

"It happens in this canyon. Time slips by," Dan said.

Lorelei laid down close to her stepfather on a pallet she had been sleeping on for weeks. Only now she did not sleep. Her mind raced as did her heart. She could hear the pounding in her ears. Her life upended when her mother and stepfather decided to leave the tenant farm she had known for years. She had been old enough to stay behind. She could have even managed a marriage to a boy that courted her although she found him humorless and prone to stomach ulcers.

Once again, her life upended when they buried her mother on an open prairie. Now, in this canyon she found her future. She could have never imagined it would be with a Cherokee cowboy. She curled up in her blankets against the chill and stared out at the animals in the clearing. The horses stood silent. The bull, cow, and calf laid down close to each other. They were all bathed in moonlight, the pinto's black and white spots standing out from the rest.

Dan looked out at the stock in the moonlight as well. He sat quietly in the dying fire light smoking a pipe. He watched the gray with the number forty branded low on its forearm. Turning a thought over and over in his head. Finally, he gently tapped the pipe bowl on a wagon wheel and set the pipe aside.

Levi snored as he was the only person in the camp a sleep. The other three laid awake. Each plotting their own future.

Chapter 14

––––◆"◆"◆––––

The sky turned pale blue and light from the east streaked over the rim of the canyon. Levi and Turon led the horses down to water. Standing along the little stream below where the spring ran from the rock, Levi turned to Turon in surprise.

"You are going to what?" Levi said in disbelief.

"I am going to marry Lorelei," Turon repeated.

"You took longer picking a bull." Levi shook his head.

"I had forty bulls to choose from then. She is the only woman in this canyon. Makes the choice easier," Turon said with a grin.

"Does she know this or are we going to break her to lead like the bull and mares?" Levi asked incredulously.

"She knows. I will ask her stepfather after breakfast," Turon said.

"Least we will have full stomachs when he runs us off with that rifle of his," Levi said.

They staked the horses back in the clearing. As they walked to the camp Lorelei set a cast iron oven of biscuits away from the coals. Using salt pork drippings and lard she browned flour in a skillet. Adding some milk, she made gravy and announced breakfast was almost ready.

They gathered around and ate. Dan talked between mouthfuls of gravy and biscuit. Levi ate the biscuits with butter and accepted the honey. He managed to avoid the gravy and salt pork. Although hunger had forced him to eat the cured pork of the region he tried to still be kosher as much as possible. He couldn't deny that the salt and sugar cures used in pork preservation tasted good, which led him to question this part of his faith but only as long as his hunger lasted. On a full stomach he became more devout.

With breakfast over Lorelei cleaned up the dishes. She carried them to the stream to wash only after giving Turon a long look. Dan stood up and grabbed a leftover biscuit.

"I reckon you'll be leaving soon," he said taking a bite of biscuit while looking toward Lorelei as she washed the plates.

"Mr. Conner, I would like to marry Lorelei." Turon stood before the towering man.

For a few moments it was silent. Levi looked on at the two men. Dan looked intently at Turon. Turon matched his stare waiting for a response.

The nervous Levi stood slowly.

"I will saddle the horses," Levi said, sensing this would not go the way Turon planned it and relieved to be on their way.

"Hold up there, Little Kansas," Dan's deep voice commanded. "What does Lorelei have to say about this?" Dan said still staring at Turon.

"I say yes." Lorelei returned with a stack of plates and utensils.

"Any man who would save his money and travel nearly seven hundred miles to buy a bull to better himself isn't rakish or a degenerate," Dan said. "You have my blessing and may God bless this union."

Lorelei went to him and hugged the man who had loved her mother. He had married a poor widow, one rumored to be Cherokee, and took a daughter on to raise loving and caring for her as if she were his own.

Tears developed and a few streaks ran down her face. Dan took Turon's hand in his own and they shook, callus to callus, looking into each other's eyes. In that moment Dan surrendered that of his earlier life and Turon Turtle agreed to care for and protect his daughter.

Levi stood dumbfounded slowly shaking his head from side to side.

"What's wrong, Little Kansas?" the deep voice of Dan asked.

"This country," Levi said. "You need a job? Here, catch this cow. Need a horse? Here is a mustang on the prairie. Need a wife? Here is this canyon," he added, still shaking his head in disbelief.

"You need a wagon?" Dan asked Levi.

"Wagon?"

"Here, here is a wagon. You are going to need a freight wagon if you are to trade in the Nations." Dan said with a sweep of his arm. "By rights what is in the wagon is Lorelei's by way of her mother. The wagon is mine. It's a good wagon. Old but good. Studebaker makes them stout."

"What do you propose?" Levi asked.

"I propose, I'll trade you this wagon and harness for that gray horse and fifty dollars." Dan lifted a finger to the gray. "On conditions, however. You help tote Lorelei's possessions to her new home. The mule I give to Lorelei as a wedding present."

All stood silent. Levi was taking it all in.

Turon was the first to break the silence. "Well, Little Kansas, what do you think?"

"This country." Levi simply said then stepped to

Dan who towered over him.

"I will trade." Levi took the tall man's hand.

"See they make it to their home safe. You have made a great journey coming here from Poland. You have seen things most of us have not. Good luck building a store." Dan pulled Levi close as he shook the immigrant's hand.

Dan turned to the wagon where he began pulling out his personal belongings and setting them to the side. Turon walked to where he had just placed a change of clothes and a wool coat.

"You're welcome to come with us," Turon said as Lorelei came to stand by him. "We can find a place for you. Benton County is across the line. It is not far and there is work."

"Thank you for the offer. However, I'm finished with Arkansas and there would be no place for me in the Nations," Dan said. "I am no preacher or teacher. I don't intend to marry again. They would not let me stay and ever own anything of my own." Dan placed a hand on Turon's shoulder. "You were right about the Cheyenne or soldiers coming soon. There are signs in this canyon of fall hunts. It's only a matter of time before someone finds us here."

Tears ran down Lorelei's face and Dan reached out and held her briefly.

"Don't cry, little girl. You've been a good daughter. Now is your time to be a good wife."

Dan let the girl loose and turned his attention to Turon. "That pinto looks like he could pull a wagon. Is he harness broke?"

"He will be by the time we get to the Cherokee Nation."

Dan continued to gather gear, stuffing items into a canvas bag. Lorelei prepared a sack of food for him to take. She stuffed a partial sack of flour in the bottom, as well as salt pork, a tin of lard, and the remaining coffee.

From the wagon Dan took out a well-oiled saddle. Spreading a blanket, he laid out his rifle and a revolver of the same caliber. Also, a large knife, hatchet, box of forty-five caliber cartridges, tobacco, and assorted items important to him.

Levi walked to the clearing and caught the gray. He patted the side of the horse's neck and rubbed his head.

"You saved my life once," he said softly and then led the gray close to the wagon and tied him to an oak sprout.

"You can have the bridle and bit," he said to Dan. "It fits him well."

"Thank you, Little Kansas. There's a box in the wagon that has books in it. They go with the wagon." Turning to Lorelei he raised his voice a little. "Hear that, Lorelei? See he gets my box of books."

"Yes sir," she said as she rearranged the wagon.

Thinking of the fifty dollars, Levi pulled a worn leather wallet from his waist. He counted out fifty and tucked the rest back in place. Handing the money over to Dan, he asked, "Do you have paper to write a bill of sale?"

Dan's deep voice sounded. "No one will question the ownership of this horse. I will give you one on the wagon. You may need it for a loan to build a store."

Levi suddenly felt concern for Dan and origins of the gray horse worried him. "Where will you go?"

"New Mexico. Maybe Arizona Territory," Dan replied.

This eased Levi's worry.

Turon led the remaining mule to the wagon along with the pinto.

"That mule will work best as the left wheeler," Dan told Turon.

Nodding, Turon soon had the mule harnessed and in place. He was a fine mule. Taller than the pinto his coat of hair was bay with darker hair on his points. The pinto stood for the harness but eyed the wagon with suspicion.

Turon hooked the team to the wagon. He attached the single trees to the double tree and hooked the trace chains in place. Raising the wagon tongue, he hooked the neck yoke to both the mule and pinto. The pinto stood still but eyed the whole apparatus. The calm professional mule waited for a command which calmed the pinto.

Levi transferred his saddle to Turon's bay since Turon said he would drive the wagon until he was convinced the pinto would behave himself. Dan had saddled the gray. He tied a canvas bedroll behind the saddle. Two bags hung on either side of the pommel and a leather strap fastened to his rifle hanging from the horn and pointing downward.

Turon caught up the cow's lead rope and tied it to the back of the wagon. He did likewise with the bull tying him beside the cow. The calf who was well on to being three months old would be able to keep up. Turon let him run loose knowing he would not stray far.

Levi had the mustang mares tied head to tail. Their colts, already acquainted with the calf, trotted and ran amongst the caravan of travelers as they prepared to go.

Dan stood up from where he had been sitting and drinking the last of the morning coffee and slapped his thigh.

"Well, guess that's it. Nothing left to do. And we've said all our goodbyes."

He gently took Lorelei by the shoulders and looked deeply into her eyes. "Make your mother proud."

Her eyes watered and she embraced him.

Dan looked at Turon. "Do me a favor. Find a preacher when you can."

"We will," Turon said.

Levi took his turn and shook hands with the tall Dan and looked up at him. "If you get in a fix, give the gray his head. He is smart, he has bottom. He will not quit."

A large hand clasped Levi's right shoulder.

"Good luck, Little Kansas," the tall man said.

"You can post a letter to the Oaks Lutheran Mission, Indian Territory. Someone there will get it to us," Turon said.

"I'll write as soon as I know where I'm going." Dan stepped up into the saddle.

His weight was greater than that of Levi's, but the gray did not seem to mind the new rider. Removing his battered trail beaten hat Dan made an arching sweep with it, bid farewell, and urged the gray west. Riding toward his future. Leaving behind all he had known.

Lorelei watched him ride away. Her future lay to the east; with a man she had known for less than sixteen hours. A man, a bull, and a nervous little man who talked funny. She turned her back on her stepfather and walked to the wagon. Turon offered a hand to her as he had seen other men do with women. She accepted his hand although she was capable of climbing into a wagon seat.

Turon handed her his rifle, and she placed it nearby beside her shotgun. He walked over to Levi and asked, "Ready, Little Kansas?"

"I'm ready. I saw a doe and this year's fawns earlier down the canyon. You want me to take them too?" Levi grinned.

"This cowboying has turned you into a smart-ass,

Little Kansas," Turon said.

"I'm ready. If the pinto breaks into a run, I'll be there to catch his head," Levi said with a serious tone.

"I think he will be fine but be ready." Turon nodded and climbed into the wagon seat. Lorelei sat close. They looked at each other for a moment. Turning to the mismatched team he flipped the leather reins across the backs of the mule and pinto.

"Step up, mule, step up, step up there," He spoke to the animals.

The mule stepped out. The forward tug the mule created pulled the wagon with a jerk. The pinto stepped out too but at a faster pace than the mule. The trace chains tightened and released as the pinto lunged against the collar and his share of the load only to fall back placing the load of the wagon onto the shoulders of the mule. Soon the pinto learned to pull with the mule for every time he tried this trick Turon would flick the leather rein in a way that slapped his rump.

It was in this manner they left the canyon, Turon talking to the mule and pinto in a teamster's tone and picking his way through rocks and trees. Then he switched to a more conversational tone when he and Lorelei spoke. The bull and cow followed the wagon obeying the ropes. Levi brought up the rear trailing the mustang mares. The colts and calf kept pace. Occasionally Levi checked their back trail for he had not forgotten the Cheyenne who had threatened to steal the bull.

Chapter 15

———◆«◆»◆———

The first day they traveled twelve miles before Turon decided to make camp. The pinto was finishing the day better than he had started. He had learned that keeping the trace chains tight made the work easier. That way he and the mule shared the load of the wagon.

Turon remarked on this during many of the talks he and Lorelei had.

"Reminds me of what an old man once told me about marriage," Turon said.

"What does a mule and spotted horse have to do with marriage?"

"He said the secret to a good marriage was to keep the trace chains tight," Turon explained. "When we left this morning, the pinto kept trying to slow down or speed up. This caused the mule strain and unnecessary work. Also caused us to go this way and that way. Now they are working together, and the load is easier. They are also traveling in a straight line."

Lorelei smiled. "I will keep the traces tight." She placed an arm on his.

"So will I."

Ahead of them was a little stand of cottonwoods along the creek that flowed north. Turon indicated with a thumb that they should stop and give the stock a chance to water and graze.

"This mule has not worked in six weeks. The pinto has had a good day," Turon said.

Lorelei agreed and when Turon stopped the wagon near an ancient cottonwood she quickly scrambled down and helped with the team. Levi rode up assessing the situation and led the mares to water. With the efficiency of someone accustomed to trail travel, Lorelei gathered wood being cautious of rattlesnakes near fallen branches.

Lorelei built a fire. As it burned, she grabbed two feed bags that had a mix of oats and corn. Without consulting the men, she first gave the mule his share hanging the bag's strap behind his ears. She patted the mule and thanked him. The ugly pinto snorted at her as she approached. She calmly walked to him softly saying sweet words. She lifted grain so he could sample it. As it was to his liking, he allowed her to place the feed bag on his head, and he chowed down on the grain.

"She will spoil that horse," Turon said turning to Levi who was rubbing down the bay's back.

"She will spoil me if she makes biscuits again," Levi said as he curried the horse's rump.

After tending to the horses Levi took a walk with his shotgun. A prairie chicken soon flushed, and he brought it down firing the sixteen-gauge shotgun. Reloading quickly, he walked to where the bird fell, and another one took flight only to crumble to the earth after his shot.

As the evening drew near Lorelei did spoil them with more biscuits, and she roasted the two birds. Although a simple meal, it was filling.

The animals grazed while there was an opportunity. Both the horses and cattle needed to eat at least two percent of their weight in grass a day just to keep their body condition. Animals on the trail moved farther and burned more energy than those who lounged in a pasture. So, they would need to eat twice that depending on how far they walked in a day's time.

The summer was over. As the grass grew and seed heads developed, the nutrient rich grasses would soon go dormant, drawing back the nutrients to the roots to insure next year's growth. The mature stalks with their seed heads held mass but lacked the nutrients needed to keep animals on the move in a healthy condition.

The seasoned prairie traveler knew these things. Turon learned from cattlemen like Mr. Hatcher how to push animals to achieve distance while also keeping them in condition even gaining weight. People unfamiliar with these things would drive animals hard allowing little time for rest and recuperation. Those people killed horses. And, sometimes forced to walk on the prairies, killed themselves in the process.

"I think Lorelei can handle the team," Turon said after supper. "I'll saddle that dun mare in the morning."

"Driving a wagon too dull for you?" Levi asked.

"The dun will be worth more if she's broke to ride," Turon said. "Before it's over she might need to take a turn in the harness."

"I could do the same with the roan. Could at least saddle her and get her used to it," Levi said seeing the merit of it.

The next morning, they saddled the dun. She humped up against the weight of the saddle, but she let the men hold and pull the cinch tight. Levi climbed on the bay and took a dally around the horn pulling the dun's nose close to his side.

"They can't buck if they never learn how. Keep her head up. We will lead her a while," Turon said.

With the team hitched and the bull and cow tied in place Lorelei started the wagon north and east on a route Turon had suggested.

While Levi held the dun's head high, Turon stepped into the saddle. The dun took the weight. She made several short jumps, but Levi urged the bay forward and he tugged the dun along. She soon walked beside the bay. Levi loosened the dally to give her some slack and she soon walked as if she ignored the burden.

They did this for a while until Turon asked for Levi to turn loose of the lead line. The dun continued to follow the bay. Turon pulled back on the rope halter, and she stopped. He stepped from her, and she lunged sideways although she did not go anywhere once the rope halter tightened.

"She will be fine. I will work with her again later." Turon handed the lead rope to Levi.

Turon then trotted up beside the wagon and jumped onto the side climbing over to sit beside Lorelei.

"Good way to get run over," she said.

"Some jumps are worth the risk." He smiled.

Turon rode the dun mare the next morning. She tried to buck but Turon stayed on, and she gave up the effort. He rode out in front of the wagon when he topped a hill. The others came to the crest and looked out to see where Turon had been gazing.

Below them ran the Cimarron. It moved like a giant serpent coming out of the plains. Between them and the river, open prairie still existed. Across the river and along the ninety-eighth meridien to the east fences had started going up. One hundred-and sixty-acres lots.

Families grew corn and fenced out neighbor's

cows, hogs, and horses. Sod houses and tents dotted the landscape.

"Maybe we could go around it all," Levi suggested.

"It would take too long," Turon said. "The river runs east from here more or less. Forty miles to the Iowa, Sac and Fox reservations."

"How many miles to your home?" Lorelei asked.

"Hundred and seventy maybe," Turon said.

"Twelve days?" Levi asked.

"More like fifteen," Turon said.

"The quickest and easiest way will be to stay on the south side of the river. All the way to the Arkansas. After we cross it there are ferries at the Verdigris and Grand rivers," Turon said. "The Chisholm Trail is east a little way. Them old moss horns would have a tough time getting through those barbed wire fences now." A hint of regret sounded in his voice. He had never been on a big trail drive.

"Momma is buried just south of there," Lorelei said.

"We have time if you would like to visit," Levi offered.

"No." She shook her head softly. "She's not there anymore."

Levi pondered this statement. Thinking she must mean she is in heaven or a spirit. They sat quiet for a few moments. Then Turon urged the dun forward. Lorelei rode the brake as the wagon eased down the slope. Levi looked once again to the west over the last of the open wild country. Then he turned and followed making up the rear guard of the little caravan.

The last several days they could have been the only people on earth. Now they descended into civilization sprouting and clawing its way from the plowed prairie. Taking everything natural in its consumption.

CHAPTER 16

———◆«◆»◆———

Farm after farm they passed. Several times dogs came out to bark at them as they made their way along the road paralleling the river but usually retreated after a sharp tongue lashing from Turon or Levi.

Turon returned to the wagon seat after a little dog got under the team and managed to nip the pinto's hind leg. Unfortunately, for the dog, a hoof caught it, flinging the dog into the wagon tongue, and it limped away yelping.

Section roads were open at mile intervals. This made for a straight shot across the country till the river swung south and they only had to go one more section before they were able to continue east.

There were places where the road was boggy and sows with pigs wallowed. People built sod houses or put up tents close to the roads. Many waved as they went by. Few stopped to talk. Most would stop work and look the group over for any familiar faces. When not finding any, they returned to their toil.

Although the road made for easy travel, they were no longer in grass country. Five months earlier it had all been open prairie. However, now where they traveled most of the prairie was plowed under. Milk cows and plow horses ate what grass was handy along the road.

Turon worried about pushing the stock too far, too fast. Finally, where the river made its most southern bend they found a place to camp. Not wishing any trouble they kept to themselves along the river. But there was hardly enough grass for the stock.

The next day in the afternoon where Cottonwood Creek emptied into the Cimarron, they saw the new town of Guthrie. Where tents and sod houses stood on the surrounding farms a great brick and block city was thrusting upwards.

"Queen of the prairie it is called," Lorelei said. "That tallest building is a bank." She pointed out the massive structure under construction.

"It has got nothing on Tahlequah on a Saturday," Turon said with disdain.

A train whistle blew in the distance. Before the locomotive was visible, they saw black smoke rising from the engine. Then the train pulled into the Guthrie station.

"Hard to believe nothing was here five months ago," Levi said.

"Cattle were here. Before that Indians were," Turon said with a growing distaste for the place he currently viewed. "Let's go around it. We don't need anything from there."

He turned the team south and found a trace going east. He pushed the team harder than he usually did. The wagon roads were well worn in and out of Guthrie. By late in the day, they crossed the line onto Iowa tribal land. The fences were gone, and prairie opened before them. Most of the Iowa tribe lived near and around Iowa Village to the south.

The creek where they stopped offered little more than some water for the stock and grass. Stumps from recently cut trees stood up and down the creek bank. Drag marks and deep ruts of wagon tracks leading off to the newly formed Oklahoma territory told the story.

"They ain't satisfied with what they got so they got to come here and take more," Turon said.

Levi had not seen this side of Turon very much. Since coming across the land run homesteads, he had become morose. Levi only hoped he would return to his old self the closer they got to the Cherokee Nation.

"This was Seminole land a few decades ago. It all was from here to the Texas Panhandle." Turon waved his hand to the west. "They will come for the Cherokee land, Little Kansas. Not just the Outlet, but all of it."

"Maybe not, maybe they will have enough," Levi said trying to comfort his troubled friend.

"If they can build that fast out on this prairie, what will they accomplish where there is timber and stone?" Turon asked.

"We will cross that creek when we come to it," Levi said borrowing a quote from Turon himself.

Turon smiled. "You are right. No need to worry until something happens."

It was then that Lorelei announced supper.

After the meal Levi was feeling bold and wanted to tease Turon in hopes the fun might improve his spirits.

"Lorelei, if Turon doesn't find a minister soon I might have to marry you myself," Levi said. "I haven't eaten this good since Chubb had his quail trap."

"I should have found a preacher in Guthrie. I did promise Dan I would find one," Turon said.

"Tulsey Town has a minister," Levi said remembering a church there.

"Too bad Preacher Bob isn't with us," Turon said.

"Who's Chubb and Preacher Bob?" Lorelei asked.

This got Turon started, and he told stories from their days cowboying on the Outlet. The time a cow ran

Preacher Bob up a tree and his horse ran off. When the horse came back to cow camp, the hands all spread out looking for the Bob fearing he had fallen. When they finally found him, he was still in the tree and the cow still eying him. Bob was delivering a sermon to the cow who, he said later, needed religion.

"There was that time John Boiling thought he had been snake bit," Levi said.

"Turned out to be red wasps that got into his bedroll." Turon chuckled. "John had given all his possessions to his brother Jeff and asked Frank to write his mother a letter before we realized what had happened," Turon explained.

The stars were shining when Turon and Levi wound down the storytelling. Lorelei made her a pallet to sleep on near the wagon under the canvas tarp that kept the dew from falling on her. Nearby Turon and Levi spread their bedrolls along the tarp's edge. Near enough for the tarp to shed dew but far enough to respect proprieties.

The following day they met very few people. All were Sac and Fox. Mostly hunting and one with a small flock of sheep. Levi had a strong urge to trade for a lamb. He had not seen many sheep in the region. He had not eaten lamb since leaving Poland and the memory made him homesick.

They traveled on. The land became flat on the south bank of the Cimarron. Signs of earlier floods remained as driftwood sometimes laid several hundred yards from the water's edge. A few times they found buffalo skulls sticking up from the sand and clay. Remains exposed by rushing water now baked by the sun. Stopping to inspect one such skull Levi picked up a stone point.

"Look at this." He held the flint point aloft.

Turon rode up and took it turning it over in his hand. As long as his hand was wide, it still held an edge capable of cutting. On both sides the flint point had been fluted leaving a long groove on either side.

"Looks like it could have been made last week, but it is old," Turon said.

"How old?" Levi asked.

"Older than the Osage. From a people long ago. Maybe the first people," Turon said.

Turon handed it back and Levi ran a thumb along the point's edge. "The last person who held this could have been the person who made it."

"Could be." Turon agreed. "Stick it in your saddle bag. It is a token, might bring good luck or when you are old you can hold it, and it will remind you of this place."

CHAPTER 17

––––––◆ "◆" ◆––––––

Six days they traveled from the Queen of the Prairie until they came to Mann's Ford on the Cimarron River. Mann's Ford had been a popular crossing on the river for decades. The firm bottom of the river at this point made for a safer crossing. Elsewhere along the river, crossing a wagon was risky. In places sand moved as freely as the water, providing no place for an animal in harness to find footing or a wagon wheel to turn. In other places red clay mud coated the horse hoofs and clung to wagon wheels. The added weight to animals and wagon became too much, bogging down the wagon in mire and drowning the animals.

They had no major river crossings with the wagon or bull so far. Lorelei and her family used well established ferries on their trip west. Now they faced two river crossings in as many miles at the confluence of the Cimarron and Arkansas. Once across Cimarron they would have to cross the Arkansas to continue their trip east. To go down river and cross only the Arkansas would mean losing a day or even two days of travel. To cross each river here at this point also meant crossing two lesser rivers. Once the red muddy Cimarron mingled with the more sedate Arkansas, they created a wide tricky river. Three quarters of a mile wide in places. Water could be seven inches deep or seventeen feet deep depending on rainfall in the over one hundred thousand square miles of country the two rivers drained.

They made camp in a walnut grove. Lorelei gathered the fallen balls of fruit. She laboriously removed the husks. Once she had what she considered enough she cracked the inner shell and dug the sweet nuts out to use for making a candy dish. Turon and Levi picketed the stock so they could graze and gave the mule and pinto the last of the grain.

"I will take the bay across the ford and scout the Arkansas. See how the crossing is there," Turon said.

Levi did not object to this. Choosing a crossing was a crucial decision. Turon had more experience reading the currents than he did.

"The pinto has a loose shoe," Levi said while pointing to the horse eating his ration of grain. "I will tend him and restitch the mule's collar."

Turon nodded and caught the bay. He soon rode out across the ford.

Levi took to fixing the collar and making minor repairs to the harness while the pinto ate his feed. It was after all his to repair. He thought daily of little improvements he would make to the wagon once they were at Turon's home place. The wagon was to become his livelihood. His home.

He finished the harness repair and addressed the pinto's loose shoe. Replacing some nails, he reset the shoe. Using the claw end of the hammer, he twisted the nails to the right breaking off the points. He then bent the nail using a rasp and clincher tool. Hammering the nail end into the hoof wall he did not notice the rider at the edge of camp.

"Good day, friend," a voice said startling Levi.

Levi let the pinto's hoof down and looked up at a man sitting on a thin sorrel mare. The man was lean with a scar running along his jawbone. His hat looked newer than the black coat he wore but it did not fit well. A little big for his head. It would more than likely fall off if the sorrel broke into a run. Only the sorrel mare did not look like she had a run in her.

"Howdy, what can I do for you?" Levi said looking around trying to see where Lorelei was.

"I saw your woman gathering walnuts. Do what I say, and no harm will fall upon her," said the man.

"What is it I should do?" Levi asked.

Pulling a revolver from under his coat he pointed it at Levi's belly.

"First, you drop that hammer." He motioned with the barrel of his gun.

Levi let the hammer fall to the ground.

"Now take that saddle and saddle your best horse."

"My best horse?" Levi asked.

"It ain't that jug-headed Indian pony you were just working on," the man said.

"The strawberry roan is the best horse I own," Levi said.

This was the truth. Levi only owned the strawberry roan mare and her colt. The roan had learned to stand while being saddled but the rest of her manners were awful. She had managed to throw Levi once and almost one more time. A person could ride her, if that person could stay on the first five minutes.

"Then saddle her, kid. I'm partial to roans anyhow," the man said. "Do exactly what I say, and I'll leave you this saddle and pony in trade."

Levi eyed the saddle. It was a type he had seen vaqueros' ride. This one was well worn. Levi caught the roan and led her to the wagon. He placed a blanket on her back then his saddle. She paid no attention to this process as she had the half dozen other times. Levi started to reach into the wagon for a bridle, but the man's gun came up.

"The bridle is in the wagon bed." Levi eyed the gun.

"Move slow then. Come out with anything other than a bridle and your blood will soak this ground," the man said.

Levi moved slow. He retrieved the bridle and looked at the shotgun in the wagon but left it in place. Stepping to the roan she allowed him to slip the bridle on only showing a little resistance to the bit.

"Take that sack and stuff it with food. Beans, flour, salt pork, or whatever you got," the man said while still sitting on the worn-out sorrel.

Levi did as commanded. Even tied the sack to the saddle.

"What kind of guns do you have?" the man asked.

"Shotgun in the wagon," Levi said.

"No rifle?" the man asked.

"No, just the shotgun."

"You have a fancy outfit. Minus that ugly horse. That's a high bred bull over there." The man jerked his head toward the Hereford. "How much money you have on you?"

Levi watched the barrel of the revolver. He finally answered. "Two hundred dollars."

"You had two hundred dollars. Where's it at?" the man asked.

Levi said his waistband and pulled out the worn leather wallet.

"Put it in the sack." The man pointed to the sack hanging on the roan's saddle.

As Levi complied his blood was beginning to boil. He did not like this. He hoped Lorelei would stay away and not get involved. At the same time, he desperately wanted Turon to ride in to camp.

"Kid, I want you to sit down against that wagon wheel. If you move, I'll kill you." The man stepped off the sorrel mare.

Levi sat down. Rage simmered within him, but he dared not do anything while that revolver pointed at his midsection. He felt clever saddling the roan. Beside the wagon and old shotgun this man was about to ride off with everything he owned. The money made him mad. He needed that money to start his business. He had two chances. Getting to the shotgun or that roan had better buck.

"As agreeable as you have been I wish I could stay and meet your woman. See if she is also agreeable." The man climbed onto the roan, his expression looking sinister.

Levi's blood boiled at that comment. His muscles tightened and his head began to ache.

The man urged the roan toward the river crossing. Riding about thirty feet he tucked the revolver under his coat.

Levi was incredulous. The roan stepped out like a well-bred saddle horse. Turning in the saddle the man shouted back to Levi. "Looks like I am getting a colt, too."

After saying this the man drummed his heels to encourage the roan into a lope. It was then the roan had enough of the rider and the direction she was traveling. Jerking her head down she pulled the reins from the man's grip, and he scrambled to gain some leverage over her head. Feeling her burden off balance the roan mare gathered herself and jumped high then kicked her hind legs even higher. Using her head and momentum of the kick she dumped her rider forward to where he fell to the ground. The man hit hard; his breath knocked from his lungs. The roan gathered herself for another jump and in doing so all four feet came down all around the man on the ground. The contents of the sack went flying and landed about. The roan stopped bucking and ran to the dun mare.

Levi was on his feet. He did not take time to get the shotgun. He ran straight to the man who had sat up and was starting to stand. Levi's speed and momentum caught the man off guard as Levi lowered his shoulder knocking the man backwards. Dazed, the man had no time to defend himself. Two years of work on prairies had harden this little Jewish immigrant. His fist landed hard. First on the man's already scarred jaw followed by a crushing blow to the man's nose. He then pounded the man's ribs. His fist glanced off something hard and he felt one of the man's ribs give way and move.

The gun, he thought, and pulled it from the man's coat.

Breathing hard he stood up and staggered several steps from the man lying on the ground. Levi stood for a minute breathing hard. His muscles suddenly felt weak, and he sat on the ground pointing the revolver at the man he and the roan had just beaten.

"Drop the gun," a voice from nowhere commanded.

Another one? Levi hurriedly glanced around.

"Deputy U.S. Marshal Reeves. Set the gun down, son."

Levi complied. He looked behind him to find Lorelei standing beside a tall black man with a huge mustache. The man held a rifle pointed at the criminal on the ground who started to move and moan.

Marshal Reeves walked over to Levi and picked up the revolver. He stuck it in his boot top then reached a hand down to Levi. Levi took it and the marshal lifted him one-handed to his feet while the rifle barrel still pointed at the man on the ground.

"You did a fair piece of work," the marshal said.

Lorelei rushed up and inspected Levi.

"Are you okay?"

"Yeah, just feel spun up."

"I would have been here sooner, but it looked like you were handling it," the marshal said. "Smart using that horse. Miss Lorelei said she would buck."

"He caught me off guard while I was putting a shoe on the pinto," Levi said his breathing returning to normal.

"Stay on guard when you are out here." The marshal looked toward the river.

Suddenly they saw Turon riding back, and the marshal was on alert.

"He's with us," Levi said.

"Marshal, would you stay for supper?" Lorelei asked.

"Would be an honor, Miss Lorelei. Just let me secure the prisoner." The marshal went to work tying the man's hands to either side of a small walnut tree some distance away but still within eyesight.

Turon rode in on the bay, his pants wet to the knees. His boots were hanging from a rope slung over his saddle horn and his bare feet rested in the stirrups. He took a quick look at the man secured to the tree, the marshal, and Levi.

"Get the shoe back on the pinto?" he asked calmly.

Levi nodded. "I did, then we had company."

"Turon, this is Deputy U.S. Marshal Bass Reeves. He is a friend of the family from back in Arkansas," Lorelei said excited.

Turon nodded a greeting.

"Ol' Dan and I did some horse trading now and then. Sorry I missed him," the marshal said.

"Who is that tied to the tree?" Turon asked.

"Wild Bill Kirby. Wanted for murder, horse stealing, and assaulting a clergyman," Marshal Reeves said keeping an eye on the prisoner.

"Murder?" Levi asked.

"Yes sir. Little Kansas, you thrashed one of the toughest and most dangerous men this side of Little Rock." Marshal Reeves said admiringly.

Suddenly Levi felt like vomiting.

Lorelei set about making supper. She was thrilled to have Levi safe, and no harm had come to Turon. She was also extremely happy to have a familiar face in camp. The marshal represented home.

Levi gathered up the sack of food the outlaw had started to leave with and picked up his wallet. He also unsaddled the roan and staked her back out. Turon offered to get the marshal's horse so he could stay close to the prisoner. Returning to camp Turon led a fine gray gelding. The marshal thanked him and tended to his horse.

Lorelei fixed a grand meal. As a treat she had used the walnuts, honey, and some sugar to make candied walnuts to which all the men raved about, with the exception of Wild Bill Kirby who Marshal Reeves claimed had no appetite.

They talked of the news in the Territory. Turon asked about Ned Christie and was not surprised when Marshal Reeves said he was still on the scout and avoiding capture.

"I do not think he killed Dan Maples," Turon said.

"I'm not sure he did either, but there is a warrant out for him," Reeves said.

They talked on into the evening.

"I'll ride with you all to Tulsey Town if you don't mind," Reeves said.

"We do not mind. It would be our pleasure," Turon said.

This pleased Lorelei and she appeared thrilled.

"I owe it to Dan and her mother's memory to see

you two find a preacher." Reeves looked at Turon. "I'd also like to join you all because I'd feel better having a fighting man like Little Kansas close by in case we run into any trouble."

Levi laughed but looked like he might cry soon. "I got lucky."

"You got crafty. You got to be crafty out here. Crafty and quick. You were both today," Marshal Reeves said.

CHAPTER 18

———◆«◆»◆———

Morning came and the party prepared to cross both rivers. Items the water could damage were placed higher in the wagon box. Turon assured Lorelei the water should not get much higher than the bottom of the box but better to prepare in case.

Lorelei drove the wagon, and the mule and pinto plunged into the Cimarron without hesitation or complaint. The two mismatched animals worked in unison. Turon mounted on the bay and rode ahead leading the bull and cow who obeyed the rope and followed him across. Riding the dun mare Levi led the roan and the colts and calf splashed through the water to keep up with the caravan.

Marshal Reeves held back and would bring up the rear with the prisoner Bill Kirby.

"Kirby, this will be a more pleasant trip if you refrain from conversation," Reeves told him.

The outlaw's eyes filled with hatred at the marshal, but he did not talk. His face was swollen, and he winced when he breathed too deeply, but he did not speak.

Turon and Levi took the cattle and horses across the Arkansas and turned them loose in a meadow flanked by cottonwoods. Riding the bay back across,

Turon tied ropes on either side of the wagon box and left the coils hanging in reach.

"Ready?" Turon asked Lorelei.

She nodded and flicked the leather reins across the mule and pinto's backs. They lunged forward and into the water.

"What if I fall in the water? I'll drown if I'm bound up." The outlaw Bill Kirby asked as the marshal urged the big gray into the water leading the little sorrel.

"Should have considered that before getting caught," Reeves said.

Once again, the outlaw fell silent and did not utter a word.

Lorelei talked and urged the mule and pinto forward. The water rose past the hubs of the wagon wheels and the river's force piled against the upstream side of the wagon box.

Approaching the far bank Levi splashed the dun mare into the water and met the wagon. He came in close and grabbed the rope Turon left coiled and tied. Turon did the same and the two splashed through the water ahead of the team. Both took dallies around their saddle horns and with their horses taking solid footings they pulled the wagon onto the riverbank making the burden less for the mule and pinto.

Lorelei showed relief to be across. Marshal Reeves came out onto the riverbank leading the Kirby's horse with the sullen outlaw still on.

"You did good, Miss Lorelei," the marshal said.

They rested their horses for a half hour. Lorelei repacked the wagon and Turon climbed back into the seat beside her when they started east on a well-worn wagon road toward Tulsey Town. The name came from the Muscogee word "Tulasi" meaning old town.

What now made up Tulsey Town had grown from the days the Muscogee people gathered around the giant oak that served as the council tree. The town straddled the boundary between the Muscogee and Cherokee nations. A railroad spur from the Cherokee town of Vinita that linked with Kansas City and the rest of the country provided a shipping point for cattle. Several stores now served the growing population of a thousand residents.

Late in the afternoon they arrived to Tulsey Town. Marshal Reeves excused himself and promised he would catch up with them quickly. First, he had to tend to business with the outlaw Kirby.

"Reverend Morris has the Methodist church south of here a little way. His parsonage is the small house off to the side. Tell him I sent you. He should have room for your stock. I won't be long." The marshal then led Kirby away who managed to turn and give Levi a look of hate.

A passerby recognized the outlaw and asked the marshal how he managed to catch Kirby.

Jerking his thumb Marshal Reeves motioned to Levi.

"I didn't. That gentleman did. Fighting Little Kansas took him by himself. I just happened to show up before he finished him off with Kirby's own gun," Reeves said.

Levi felt like crawling under a rock. Embarrassed by the accolades. Several men now stood and looked at Levi and then to the battered Bill Kirby.

Turon grinned.

"Mr. Kansas, should go to the Reverend Morris' place now?" Turon said in a subservient manner.

Levi was more embarrassed but managed to speak with authority.

"Move out the wagon, Mr. Turtle. We cannot stay in the street all day blocking traffic." He rode south in the direction the marshal said to go leading the horses.

"Yes, sir." Turon talked to the mule and pinto flicking the leather reins to urge them through the town traffic.

Lorelei laughed softly as they followed Levi. Townspeople watched them. Stockmen eyed the bull as he walked down the street behind the wagon as though he was the main attraction.

Dust rose from the wagon wheels and the stock as they traveled south on the dirt street. Soon they spotted a church. As they approached, they saw the parsonage off to the side. A small framed rectangular side-gabled house, the front door flanked by single pane windows.

A man sat in a chair on the porch reading the Bible. He paused and looked up when he realized the wagon had stopped. Setting the Scripture aside he stood, reached for his hat, and stepped into the sun to welcome the strangers.

"Good afternoon. Marshal Reeves said to mention he sent us," Turon said as he stepped down out of the wagon.

"Deputy Marshal Reeves is always welcome here and so are his friends," the man said.

"I am Reverend Morris." The man stuck out his hand to shake Turon's.

"I am Turon Turtle. This is Lorelei Dixon and on the bay is Levi Kuratowski."

The reverend eyed Lorelei and the wagon then Levi. Turning back to Turon he politely said, "If you are here in a professional capacity, I assume there is someone needing burial or someone needing marriage."

"We are in the marrying business," Turon said. "Miss Dixon and myself."

"I see. Miss Dixon, Mr. Turtle, are you of the faith?" Reverend Morris asked.

"Yes, Reverend," Lorelei said. "I myself am a

member of the Methodist Church in Alma, Arkansas. Turon, the Lutheran Mission at Oaks."

"One could do worse than a Lutheran, Miss Dixon," Reverend Morris said. "When would you like to have the ceremony?" he asked the couple.

"Could we have it today?" Lorelei asked.

"Are you in trouble, dear?" the reverend asked.

"No. We have been traveling for some time. Before I go another mile, I would have us go as man and wife."

"I see. We could have the ceremony now if we had another witness. Takes two witnesses," the Reverend Morris said.

Marshal Reeves rode up in time to hear their conversation.

"I will stand witness, Reverend, and give the bride away." Marshal Reeves stopped the gray horse and stepped down from the saddle. "Miss Lorelei and I are friends. I know her family. I also approve of this man." Reeves pointed a thumb at Turon.

"Good to see you, Deputy Marshal. I believe I can provide a service for your friends," the reverend said while shaking Marshal Reeves' hand.

"Is it all right if they use your vacant lots to let their stock graze for a bit?" Marshal Reeves asked the reverend.

"By all means. Help yourself. You will find a watering trough by the hitch rail." The reverend waved his hand toward a hand-pump and wooden water trough.

"Let us meet in the sanctuary in an hour," Reverend Morris said just before he and Marshal Reeves walked to the porch of the little house.

Turon drove the wagon to the edge of a vacant lot. Levi watered the horses then the bull and cow. Grass had grown knee high on the vacant lots. Turon and Levi staked the livestock out where they could graze.

Meanwhile Lorelei had disappeared into the wagon with a bucket of water and pulled the canvas closed. When she reappeared and climbed down from the wagon both Turon and Levi stared. Lorelei stood before them in a dress neither had seen. The dress was white with a pattern of little blue flowers. Her hair was tightly wrapped and lifted into a bun revealing her long slender neck.

"You may want to put on your clean clothes," Levi said to Turon while still looking at Lorelei.

Turon had no response. He ran and caught the bay, never minding saddling it. He jerked the loop from the stake driven into the ground and grabbed the bay's mane and swung on bareback. He drummed his heels into the bay's sides urging it to run down the dirt street toward the store buildings.

"Little Kansas, what did he say he was doing?" Lorelei's face held a concerned expression.

"He did not say anything."

"Is he running away?" She sounded alarmed.

"He would have taken the bull if he was leaving for good," Levi said absentmindedly. "He wouldn't run away."

An hour passed. Lorelei stood in the church to one side of the altar. The Reverend Morris stood at the front and Marshal Reeves and Levi stood on the other side.

"The young groom you vouched for appears to be missing, Deputy Marshal. We may need your tracking abilities," the reverend said solemnly.

The doors at the front of the church opened wide with a bang.

"Is there a Cherokee couple getting married today?" A man said in a loud voice.

"T.J. Archer, what brings you here?" The Reverend Morris said in a sharp tone.

Ignoring the reverend, T.J. Archer, a part Cherokee store owner walked to the front of the church.

"When he slid that horse of his to a stop in front of my store, I thought he was going to rob the place." Archer walked to Lorelei and took her by the hands.

"My dear, your man will be here momentarily. He had some quick arrangements to make. The photographer needed rousing. A carriage will be here directly to take you to your reception in the dining hall of the hotel post nuptial," Archer said with a flourish.

Before Lorelei could ask any questions the front door of the church flung open again. At the threshold Turon stood in a new suit of clothes. His pants tucked into a new pair of Heyer Olathe leather boots. On his head was a new John B. Stetson beaver hat from Philadelphia. In his hands some late summer flowers that had been hastily gathered. Onlookers and a few random cowboys followed him in.

He approached the altar with his hat in hand. Looking at Lorelei he started to speak. She hushed him and Reverend Morris cleared his throat.

The service was a short one. Long enough for propriety but short enough that the little audience did not lose focus. Marshal Bass Reeves stood in as her father and gave her away. Levi signed the certificate as witness and Reeves made his mark.

With great flourish T.J. Archer escorted the newly wedded couple out the front door where a carriage awaited. Before coming to the church Archer had lit a fire under the stable hand and motivated him to quickly get the carriage and buggy team harnessed.

Turon helped Lorelei into the carriage. Turning to Levi he spoke briefly, and Levi nodded. Turon stepped into the back seat of the carriage with Lorelei and the stable hand drove them to the hotel.

"Little Kansas is gathering our things, and he will

bring them to the hotel," Turon told her leaning close.

"You got a room?" she asked.

"When I saw you step from that wagon in this dress, I knew a wagon camp and cook fire was no place for you to spend your wedding night. I knew you deserved more than a Cherokee cowboy with holes in his trousers," said Turon.

"I like my Cherokee cowboy." She smiled.

"That is good, because you are stuck with one now."

The citizens of Tulsey Town and the hotel staff had put together a feast by the time T.J. Archer gathered the guests. He introduced Mr. and Mrs. Turtle to the growing crowd. Levi slipped into the lobby with the bags for the couple and the lobby boy carried them to their room.

Turon caught sight of Levi and forced him into the middle of the crowd.

"Here is the man who caught Bill Kirby. Beat him to the ground, he did," Turon said.

People slapped Levi on the back and pumped his hand thanking him for ridding the prairies of such a menace. Levi managed to get a plate of food and walk to a corner. Marshal Reeves came over and talked for a few minutes and wished him well before doing the same with the new married couple.

Store owner Archer summoned a fiddle player and soon people were dancing. Darkness was falling and Levi caught Turon to tell him he was going to check the stock, and he would be staying at the reverend's place.

"I want to give Lorelei time to shop in the morning. We should be able to make it to the Verdigris by sundown," Turon said.

Levi nodded then offered Turon his hand to shake. Turon took it then embraced Levi in a back slapping hug.

The people of Tulsey Town never needed much of

an excuse to celebrate. The reception drew a crowd. Women offered advice and kept referring to Lorelei as the "poor child." Men slapped Turon on the back and said, "nice work." The celebration continued even as the hotel clerk hinted that people should leave. In response to this the celebration continued. The participants celebrated so intently they did not notice that the bride and groom had slipped away to their room. The newlyweds did not mind the noise from downstairs.

CHAPTER 19

————◆"◆"◆————

Levi ate breakfast with Reverend Morris the next morning. Simple fare compared to Lorelei's biscuits, but Levi was thankful for he did not have to cook it himself. He noticed the reverend's wood pile and spent an hour splitting crosscut sections of logs into suitable sizes for the wood range in the parsonage.

Traffic along the street had picked up when Levi walked down to the stores. He wanted to see what they had in stock and take notice of what items were popular. Remembering T.J. Archer from the evening before, he walked down to his place on First Street by the Frisco railroad tracks.

Levi stepped inside the store. His eyes adjusted to the dim lighting as he glanced around the place. Farm implements, wash tubs, hardware, and bolts of cloth lined the shelves. Dry goods and barrels of flour, cornmeal, sugar, and salt sat in a line along a counter. A friendly lady's voice greeted him. She had a British accent much like Mrs. Flemming in Canadian, Texas. This woman, however, was younger and introduced herself as Mrs. Archer.

"That is Fighting Little Kansas," a more boisterous voice proclaimed.

T. J. Archer stepped from a storeroom carrying a crate and set it on a counter with a thud.

Mrs. Archer eyed Levi with interest.

"He is partnered with that young man who got married yesterday. They are cattlemen. Brought a bull all the way from Texas," Mr. Archer said. "He is also the man who single-handedly beat and apprehended Bill Kirby."

"Lawman and rancher. How fascinating," Mrs. Archer said with growing interest.

"Just a cowhand, and I got lucky with the outlaw," Levi said modestly.

"Luck follows those who will lead it," Mr. Archer said.

"Thank you, sir. I would be interested in your professional opinion on a matter," Levi said.

"Certainly, how may I be of help?"

"I would like to open a store. I have a wagon and hope to start trading in the Saline and Delaware Districts of the Cherokee Nation." Levi appeared nervous at sharing his dream.

"First, a store works better on a railroad. You will have no railroad in that area, so you need to be able to freight the goods in on a wagon," Archer said in a more serious tone. "You are on the right path by selling from a wagon. You can test your market. Get to know your customers. Know what they need, then understand what they want and can afford."

"Remember the ladies." Mrs. Archer interjected.

"Yes, bolts of cloth and practical items." Archer nodded, then added, "If you sell on credit, make sure you get collateral. A shoat pig is not worth much in August, but by December you can trade on it."

"Where do you order your goods, and can I have them shipped here?" Levi asked.

"What we cannot buy locally I have shipped in from

Kanas City. Comes on the train right to this siding."
Archer used a pencil and some package paper to
illustrate. "The problem with you having them shipped
here is your freight. You are sixty miles from here to the
Saline with two rivers to cross."

Archer marked an X on wrapping paper where Levi
wished to trade and added two lines being the Verdigris
and Grand rivers. "You could ship to Vinita, but you
still have the Grand River to cross. Your best bet would
be to ship your goods to Siloam Springs, Arkansas.
Here." He made another X. "That is maybe only twenty
miles to the Saline and right next door to the Delaware
District. Better yet, no big rivers." He put the pencil
down.

Levi studied the impromptu map.

"It is a promising idea, that area. There is
opportunity, not as good as here but there is no one in
that area that I know of who is doing business," Mr.
Archer said. "The only problem is getting a license
through the tribal council. Having a Cherokee like
Turon would help. Better yet, marry a Cherokee girl.
Then you would be all set." Archer grinned.

"I don't intend to get married anytime soon," Levi
said.

"None of us do but it happens. Happens quick for
some of us." Archer smiled at his wife.

Levi was grateful for the advice and assurance. He
felt obligated to buy something and purchased peach
preserves, and candy. He shook T.J. Archer's hand and
Mrs. Archer wished him luck.

As he walked out of the store, he heard a wagon
coming down the street. He looked up to see an old
army wagon that had a wooden enclosed box. Narrow
windows with bars bolted in place across the openings
ran down the side. A dark-skinned man, part Indian
drove the wagon. U.S. Deputy Marshal Bass Reeves

rode alongside. He noticed Levi and pulled up beside the wooden walk.

"Good morning, Little Kansas. Glad to see you managed to stay out of trouble."

"Morning, marshal. I avoid trouble when I can." Levi replied.

"Good. The way to be." The marshal turned in his saddle. "Go on ahead, Choc, I won't be long." He then turned back to Levi. "Choc and I are taking this load of prisoners to Fort Smith. Kirby made it a full load," Marshal Reeves said while Kirby glared at Levi as Choc drove the wagon down the street.

"I got word a group of men robbed a hardware store in Fort Smith. Same men robbed the payroll clerk for the Kansas and Arkansas Valley Railway in Sallisaw. The clerk was shot and killed. Track foreman shot one of the bandits. A group pursued them north out of town. They lost them near Marble City."

Levi listened intently as the marshal continued.

"Toad Scraper was one of the bandits. Frank Harper another one. He was identified by a drover in Fort Smith. He is rumored to be riding with Scraper. Turon mentioned Harper cowboyed with you all in the Outlet."

Levi nodded. He felt sick at once. Nervous.

"He got in trouble after you all left Caldwell. He beat a peace officer and stole some horses. He and some others. One was a big gray gelding that belonged to the officer." The marshal paused then continued. "It's a shame when someone you know turns bad."

Levi felt guilty and relieved he was not with Frank now.

"It's believed they will head to the Cooweescoowee district. If you see Harper stay clear of him. He may be your friend, but he is dangerous. Anyone riding with Toad Scraper for sure is dangerous. Their world is closing in around him. Better you don't get caught up in it."

"Thank you, Marshal. I will stay clear of him."

"Don't suppose you know where he might head?" The marshal asked.

"The Yukon was the last I knew. Said he planned to get rich in the gold fields."

"That's what Turon said. Well, good luck, Little Kansas. If clerking does not work out for you, come to Fort Smith. We always need good marshals." Marshal Reeves then urged his horse to catch up with the prisoner wagon.

"Marshal Kansas or Marshal Kuratowski?" Turon said walking up to Levi with Lorelei beside him. "Kuratowski is too hard to spell on paperwork. You should go by Kansas."

"You are in a good mood this morning." Levi replied.

Turon and Lorelei shared a quick glance at one another.

"I am, Little Kansas. It is a good day to be alive." Turon said with a smile.

"How about Frank?" Levi asked.

"Frank was bound to cross that line." Turon's tone was more serious now.

The three went back into T.J. Archer's store and picked up more items. After an hour of visiting and shopping they finally got back to the wagon and hitched the team. Levi was ready to go and although he liked the little cowtown of Tulsey he was ready to be on his way.

The Reverend Morris was the last to wish them luck as the caravan headed east. The bull and cow tied to the back of the wagon pulled by the mule and pinto. Following up behind rode Levi leading the horses while the colts and calf ran among the horses, wagon, and cattle.

They traveled the rest of the day across the prairie. For miles they approached a line of trees finally descending into a river bottom the early French traders named the Verdigris for its green and gray color. Quiet and deep, it rolled and cut its way south to the Arkansas. The sun was low on the horizon, so they made camp in a stand of native pecans near a creek. The bull and cow grazed as did the horses.

Lorelei made a feast for her new husband and Levi. Soon after the meal Levi suggested he would take his shotgun and stand guard for a few hours just to be sure there were no outlaws. He would be on a ridge above camp, but not too far away that if they needed him, they could yell or fire a shot.

Turon offered no protest. He remarked it was a good idea since they were in an area often traveled by highwaymen. Levi realized the importance of privacy for new couples and was not too concerned about outlaws or bandits. Neither was Turon.

CHAPTER 20

———◆«◆»◆———

The next morning the ferry operator stepped out from under a shed and watched the small group approach. He was a stout man, not much taller than Levi but with shoulders broader than Turon's. Daily he pulled on the rope strung across the Verdigris River. His hard muscles bulged below coarse black hair on his arms. Turon drove the wagon to the landing.

"Morning. I'm Blake Stone, and this is Stone's crossing," The broad man said in a deep grumbling voice.

"Morning. I am Turon Turtle. This is my wife Lorelei and that's Fighting Little Kansas in the back with the horses."

"A man came through yesterday saying that name. He caught Bill Kirby he said, beat him to a pulp." The ferry operator looked back at Levi.

"That is him," Turon smiled at Levi. "We need to cross the river if you are accepting customers this early." Turon turned back to the ferry operator.

"We are open, always open. Twenty-five cents for team and wagon with occupants. Horse and rider fifteen cents. Horses ten cents a head. Cattle three cents a head. How about seventy-five cents?" the burly operator said looking over the animals. "Cut you a deal on the colts and calf."

"Beats swimming." Turon fished six bits from his pocket.

"Safer. A Missouri man didn't want to pay back in the spring. He tried to cross his wagon. He and his team made it. But the wagon box floated off the frame, and his wife and child were swept downstream. We never found them." The ferry operator said looking at the river. "The water looks calm enough but there are holes and sucks that will swallow an elephant. We will cross the wagon and cattle first. Shorten your lead ropes so that the bull and cow will not rock the vessel." He dropped the ramp that led onto a flat bottom river boat.

Turon did as directed then drove the wagon down the ramp and onto the ferry. It was a flat bottom rectangular watercraft, built by Stone himself. Low sides around the boat made of planks kept the water from coming over the platform. A single rail waist high would not hold an animal if it decided to go over the side but it gave the illusion of security.

The river looked calm, and the ferry operator closed the ramp. Taking a long pole, he shoved off the bank and pushed against the pole until he was well in the channel. A rope ran through iron rings along the upstream side of the ferry. Dropping the pole in a rack built into the railing the ferry man walked to the front of the ferry and took a grip on the rope. Slowly he pulled overhand, and the ferry moved as bulging forearms pulled the rope through the rings to the other side of the river. The rope tied to a tree held the weight of the craft against the constant current. The pinto stood in the harness but stomped on the wood plank floor of the craft raking it with a front hoof.

"What would happen if the rope broke?" Lorelei asked.

"Now ma'am, that would be something, wouldn't it?" The ferry operator didn't elaborate.

Steadily Stone pulled the rope until the ferry made landing. He dropped the ramp on the land side of the flat bottom boat and Turon drove the team and wagon off onto the eastern bank of the Verdigris. The calf that had stayed close to its mother hesitated at the end of the ramp. He blew snot from his nostrils and jumped the transition as if he were jumping from death itself.

The ferry operator closed the ramp and shoved off back to the western bank for Levi and the horses. They had a rougher trip. The roan reared and danced around causing the ferry boat to rock. Levi shortened the lead rope, and the evenly tempered bay stood firm. The colts snorted and spun around kicking at the ferry operator as he pulled the craft back across.

"They do not like his smell. He is fishy. These river men eat a lot of fish," Turon told Lorelei.

By the middle of the river the roan had calmed down and stood still. The colts had retreated from the sharp tongue of the ferry operator Stone. When the ramp lowered Levi rode onto the bank with horses following close. The colts in turn snorted and leaped from the ramp, hooves slipping until one of them fell into a cloud of dust at the water's edge. He recovered quickly bucking as he ran away from the river monster.

"You all be safe," the river man yelled then took up a seat in the shade waiting on another customer.

The river turned and ran northeast for six miles before turning south again. Along this route walnut and native pecan trees grew in the rich bottomland. Sticks and other debris hung in branches several feet above their heads.

"The water gets that high?" Levi asked in disbelief.

"It can. About every spring it gets out of its banks. Rolls muddy and wide when it does." Turon confirmed what was obvious hanging in some of the branches.

Where the river turned south, they entered prairie land once again. They passed herds of cattle grazing, and the bull bawled his challenges but obeyed the rope tied to the wagon. They traveled eastward. Occasionally they saw a house or shack. Mostly cattle grazed on prairies but in the creek bottoms Cherokee families grew corn and large gardens. Some farms were long established with fruit trees and grape vines. They saw herds of hogs. Not wild because the male hogs were castrated and all ear marked. Each farm had their own identifying mark cut into a pig's ear showing who the owner was.

The farther east they traveled the farms became fewer. More cattle grazed on the open range. Near sundown they came to a little creek flowing off to the southeast. Turon called it Chouteau Creek and said it emptied into the Grand River.

"Better we cross it now because it gets deep near the river," he said.

"Are we getting close to your home?" Lorelei asked.

"The day after tomorrow we will be home. Just one more river to cross," Turon said.

"How far to the river?" Levi asked.

"Seven miles or eight. Not far."

In the fading light they made camp. Lorelei fixed supper while Turon and Levi watered and staked the livestock. Levi thought he saw light in the distance to the east. Turon saw it too, and now it was gone although a thin line of smoke rose from where they had seen the fire light. Soon darkness fell and they could see nothing.

"Someone does not want us to see their cook fire." Turon said in a soft voice.

"It is strange." Levi agreed.

"More than likely, they know we are here." Turon

said looking to the east.

"Who could it be?" Levi wondered aloud.

"Could be anyone, anyone who does not want to be noticed." Turon looked at the wagon.

"We should take turns sleeping." Levi suggested.

"Yeah, better load buckshot in your sixteen-gauge."

"Might be rustlers. There are cows about." Levi reasoned.

"Could be." Turon said while scanning the horizon.

"We could wait for good dark, move the wagon a few miles." Levi said weighing their options aloud.

"On this prairie we will stick out too much. No place to hide except along the creek. With the noise we would make they could hear us, but we could not hear them."

"Stay put and stand guard," Levi affirmed.

Turon did not want to alarm Lorelei but after the meal he put out the fire with some shovelfuls of dirt. He explained his precautions. She understood and looked into the darkness. By putting the campfire out, they improved their night vision. Stars shined bright in the cloudless sky. So many they appeared to hang on the horizon and above like gnats.

Levi stood first watch. He and Turon had ridden night herd. Both could tell time by the stars as easy as a man with a watch. Levi sat at the base of a hackberry tree that grew near the creek. The tree would break up his silhouette making it hard for an approaching stranger to tell where he was.

Another advantage they had were the mares. If someone approached on horseback the superior noses of the mares would pick up the scent of a strange horse. Once smelling or seeing a horse they would neigh and nicker giving way any rider who approached.

Levi grew sleepy. He slowly scanned the horizon for any unfamiliar shapes that did not belong or were new from his last scan. The shotgun laid across his lap. Turon would be sleeping with the Henry nearby and Lorelei had her double barrel shotgun.

At midnight Turon stepped over and squatted beside Levi.

"We still have all the stock." Levi said in a whisper.

"Go get some sleep."

Levi walked to his bedroll. Turon or Lorelei had rolled it out under the canvas tarp. He laid down and set the shotgun beside him pointing the barrel in a direction away from Lorelei or Turon. Sleep came but it was fleeting. He glanced at the stars about every hour. Four hours passed and he swapped places with Turon. He sat until a faint light appeared on the eastern horizon. Light that revealed two riders sitting horseback three quarters of a mile away.

CHAPTER 21

———◆«◆»◆———

Turon stood beside Levi watching the two men on horseback. He turned and looked back to the west then north and south.

"Hopefully, it is only two. If they wait and ride in when the sun is low and the brightest then we should expect trouble. They will have the advantage with the sun being in our eyes."

"They know we see them." Levi said.

Lorelei came to stand by them and peered off toward the east where the two riders still sat.

"Well, we might as well make some coffee. After we hitch the team, we can at least have a cup. If they are friendly, they will approach us once they see smoke. If they mean to harm us, then they will wait on the sun." Turon said.

"I'll start some coffee and pack while it comes to a boil." Lorelei kindled a fire.

Looking around once more to the surrounding area Turon asked Levi to hitch the team while he stood watch holding the Henry rifle. Levi moved with efficiency and did not waste any time. He led the mule and pinto to water before harnessing them. Quickly he saddled the bay and tied her to the wagon.

The sun crept up and over the horizon spilling bright light over the land. With the light came the riders. Turon and Levi each drank coffee as the riders slowly approached. Lorelei shoveled dirt over the fire and climbed into the wagon with the double barrel shotgun across her lap.

"Can you get in the wagon with Lorelei?" Turon asked Levi and tossed back the last of the coffee in his cup.

Levi nodded and took Turon's cup and his own stuffing them in a box near the back of the wagon. He set the pot in the same box before climbing into the wagon seat.

"We are too cautious. Just some cowboys hunting cattle more than likely." Levi said trying to reassure Lorelei and put her at ease.

Turon caught up the lead ropes of the mustang mares and stepped into the saddle on the bay. He slipped the mares' lead lines on the saddle horn, leaving one hand for the reins while the other held the Henry rifle.

"Let us move out southeast. Drive like you do not even see them. If they move to block our path get into the wagon box, Lorelei. Keep both barrels pointed at whichever one does the most talking."

"All right," she said simply.

"If he makes a move for a gun, fire both barrels and reload." Turon said all business.

"Maybe they will ride on." Levi said hopeful.

"Maybe, but these two don't act like citizens. They are on the run from someone. Either U.S. marshals or Cherokee authorities. Could be running from the Lighthorse in the Muscogee Nation."

Levi drove the wagon and Turon rode beside it keeping himself between the wagon and the riders. The riders stopped for a while once they saw the wagon moving out. After a moment they rode again. Only now they were angling to cut off the wagon's path. Lorelei climbed over the wagon seat as Turon told her to do and prepared to fight if necessary.

Levi balanced his shotgun in his lap while he spoke to the mule and pinto urging them southeast. This route took them along Chouteau Creek keeping it to their right. Their threat rode in from their left.

The horsemen kept their pace. Turon turned and watched behind them and across the creek to look for any more riders.

"They want to talk, whoever they are," Turon said. "Turn the wagon and head straight toward them."

"That one rider looks familiar." Levi shaded his eyes.

The riders stopped when they saw the wagon change directions. Levi kept the team headed straight for them. Two hundred yards away from the riders on a slight rise Turon told Levi to stop.

"If they want to talk let them come to us," he said.

Levi did not set the wagon brake. The mule and pinto stood where Levi stopped them.

The riders sat still for five minutes before riding forward. Slowly they walked their horses toward the wagon.

Turon, still on the bay, chambered a round in the lever action Henry rifle and left the hammer back. This made it ready to fire at any pressure of the trigger. He rested the butt of the rifle on his right thigh and the long barrel laid at rest on his right shoulder.

"You think it will come to that?" Levi asked while lifting his shotgun in the same manner.

"I hope not, but something tells me these two aren't interested in swapping candied walnut recipes." Turon watched the horsemen approach.

Levi stood and took a quick look around, sure to

scan behind them before sitting back down.

"If they ride in and split up, keep your shotgun on the one to the right." Turon said.

Looking directly at Levi, Turon spoke using Levi's real name.

"Levi, if they do mean us harm, we cannot hesitate." Turon spoke softly.

"I'd rather not kill someone, but I will, if need be," Levi replied. "You are family."

Turon nodded and turned his attention back to the two horsemen who were close enough now to make out features.

"Thats's Frank Harper on the left." Levi said in mild surprise.

"Sure, enough is." Turon couldn't tell yet if the situation would improve or worsen.

Frank and the other rider spread out and stopped about fifteen yards in front of the team. Frank looked thinner. Gray whiskers grew on his face, and he looked gaunt with hard travel. Surprise came to his haggard face as he recognized Turon and Levi.

"You missed coffee, Frank. Should have gotten around earlier," Turon said in a casual tone.

"I swear if it isn't Turon and Little Kansas," Frank said.

"Who's your friend?" Turon indicated the nervous rider accompanying Frank.

"That's Toad..." Frank started to say the full name, but Toad Scraper snapped and cut him off.

"Never mind that." Toad said in a harsh tone.

"You must be Toad Scraper. You're famous." Turon looked at the man whose eyes darted from Turon to Levi. Then to his old acquaintance, he asked, "Frank, how can we help you two? It will have to be quick for we have business across the Grand."

"You can help by tossing those guns to the ground

and stepping away from that wagon. If you have heard of me then you know what I will do." Toad gave Turon a harsh stare.

But Turon ignored him.

"Frank, I did not introduce my wife. That is her in the wagon box behind Little Kansas. Lorelei, would you please point both barrels of that shotgun at Toad. He is the one on the right with a messed-up ear."

"We need to hold up a minute," Frank said. "Turon, if you can spare some food we will be on our way."

But Toad gave a greedy look. "Food? Look how they're traveling. They got money in that wagon and fresh horses."

"They're friends, Toad. Let's go. We can get food in Vinita." Frank spoke with a hint of authority.

"Telegraph wire goes to Vinita. Word is already ahead of us. They have what we need." Toad said.

"We will find it elsewhere. No telegraph on the Osage. We can make it there," Frank said.

"Shut up, Frank."

Levi had never seen Frank ordered around like this before. He did not look like the same Frank though. This Frank had aged years in a few months.

"Stand and deliver, chief, or you lose more than a wagon and horses," Toad said looking at Turon.

"Don't push him, Toad." Frank said angrily.

Toad had freed his right foot from the stirrup and had a hold of the saddle horn with his right hand. In one motion the left-handed Toad pulled a revolver from under his coat and fell from the saddle. He brought the pistol under the horse's neck. Buckshot from both Lorelei and Levi raked the saddle seat but left Toad unharmed as he hung suspended from the horse's side, his boot still in the stirrup.

Toad's horse whirled as he fired the revolver knocking Turon from the saddle. In the excitement the mule and pinto broke into a run. Levi fell from the wagon as it jerked into motion leaving him scrambling to fall clear of the wheels.

Falling back into the wagon box Lorelei hit hard on a wooden crate. Stunned and with a sharp stabbing pain in one elbow she managed to climb over the seat. Two quick shots rang out from a revolver.

"Turon!" She screamed trying desperately to grab the fallen reins as the mule and pinto ran in flight.

The weight of the bull snapped the iron ring that tethered him to the wagon box. Free from the rope he bucked and ran from the noise then chased the wagon with the cow running to keep up.

Levi had fallen hard on his back and his head rapped the ground. Still, he was up and managed to cling to one shotgun shell. On his knees he broke open the action and shoved a new shell home into the chamber. Jerking his wrist, he snapped the action closed.

Turon laid on his back not moving. One more shot from a revolver rang out and Toad's limp body fell to the ground, his boot still in the stirrup. His horse leapt sideways before breaking into a run. The body of Toad Scraper bounced for thirty yards before it crumpled in a cloud of dust coming to rest.

Frank turned to see Levi on his feet. The immigrant cowboy held a shotgun on him. Frank held his head low and tossed the revolver onto a clump of grass and climbed off the nervous horse.

Levi quickly moved to Turon and frantically felt for a bullet wound. Frank came over and knelt beside him.

Turon tried to sit up and let out a groan.

"Are you hit?" Levi asked with concern.

"Little bastard shot me in my Henry," Turon said.

"What?" Levi asked not understanding.

"My Henry. His first bullet slammed into the rifle

then drove it into my shoulder. Feels broken," Turon said recovering quickly.

Levi inspected the rifle, and it did indeed have a dent in the magazine tube. One cartridge smashed and a streak of lead and metal on one side of the barrel. The men turned and looked at the approaching sound of the wagon. Standing with the reins in one hand Lorelei urged the mule and pinto in a run. With the other hand she held the shotgun braced against her hip. Ready to kill or be killed.

As long as he would live, Turon would never forget how she looked at that moment. Her rage and anger gave way to concern as she leapt from the wagon and ran to his side, glaring at Frank.

"I am sorry. I did not want to ride in. Didn't even want to ride with Toad but I needed enough money to get away," Frank said.

"You saved my life," Turon said. "If you had not shot him, he would have shot me."

Lorelei looked at Frank less harshly now but still held resentment.

"Lorelei, how about some breakfast and more coffee? Frank looks like he could use a meal."

CHAPTER 22

————◆«◆»◆————

Frank ate wolfishly as most cowboys did. Killing Toad did not ruin his appetite for hunger outweighed any emotional distress. Turon and Levi ate sparingly. Lorelei sipped coffee but had no desire for food as the dead body that was Toad lay in the distance.

Frank set his plate aside and held the coffee cup in two hands. "Don't suppose you have any whiskey to freshen up the coffee?"

"Sorry, no." Lorelei said sternly.

"What happened to the Boiling brothers?" Levi asked.

"Sent them home to Sarcoxie once we got away from Caldwell. Told them to stay in Missouri." Frank said before sipping the hot coffee.

"How did you end up with Toad Scraper?"

"Met him in Muskogee playing cards. A cowboy I worked with on the Cheyenne range was running with him. Sammy Higgins." Frank suddenly became quiet. "Sammy died near Marble. One of those railroad men shot him. Should have left Toad right there but he had the money."

"Hard way to make a living," Turon said.

"Toad and Sammy were doing okay. Better than

wages. I needed travel funds." Frank replied. "I didn't want to hurt anybody. It was just supposed to be banks and railroads. That hardware store rubbed me wrong. They were just working folks." Frank shook his head back and forth.

"People work at banks and railroads, too," Levi said.

"Not the same people, Little Kansas." Frank had a grain of his old self showing looking at Levi he continued. "Glad to see you got away okay."

"You nearly got me killed in Caldwell," Levi said with some rage.

"Well, you'll have that sometimes." Frank went back to his coffee.

Levi was thankful he got away from Frank when he did. He had no home to run to like John and Jim Boiling. If he had stayed with Frank, he too might be lying dead in a holler near Marble City.

"We talked to a U.S. marshal in Tulsey Town. Someone recognized you in Fort Smith. The whole Territory knows you were in on that hardware store and payroll robbery." Turon looked at Frank. "They think you are headed to the Cooweescoowee district."

Frank got up abruptly and walked away. He stood staring to the northwest for a few minutes before returning to the group.

"If they know that much then they got me nearly surrounded," Frank said in a beaten manner.

"Frank, did you kill that payroll clerk?" Turon asked firm and directly.

"No, never fired a shot until today."

"You can turn yourself in. We can take the body to Claremore. They will hold you cause Toad was Cherokee, least his mother was, but you killed him to save us." Turon said.

"The federals would get me on those other charges.

They would charge me for the payroll clerk whether I killed him or not," Frank said.

"Then what are you going to do?" Levi asked.

"Change my name for sure. I've nearly worn this one out," Frank said.

Turon stood followed by Levi. Lorelei had finished packing the breakfast dishes after cleaning them and came to stand by Turon and Levi.

"What about Toad Scraper?" She looked where the crumpled body laid.

"We bury him. We do not need any of his kin thinking we had anything to do with it. We are all okay. My shoulder is feeling better," Turon said.

Levi walked to the wagon and pulled a shovel from a pile of implements. He then started to walk to where the body of Toad Scraper.

"Little Kansas, I will do it," Frank said.

Levi stopped and Frank took the shovel.

"Just give me a little bit. I will take care of him," Frank said.

Frank went to work slicing through the tough sod with the point of the shovel. He made the hole no wider than it had to be and as long as necessary. Levi glanced at Turon holding Lorelei and did not wish to intrude on them. So, he mounted the nearby bay and rode out to gather Toad's horse and brought him back to the wagon.

Frank's horse grazed near the mares and the bull and cow were not far off. The colts and calf darted in circles in the early morning sun. Levi caught the lead ropes of the cow and bull. They both followed willingly, and he secured them to the wagon.

At Turon's urging, although she was reluctant, Lorelei made up a sack of food to give to Frank. He came back carrying the shovel with a noticeable bulge under his shirt. Placing the shovel in the wagon he then walked to Toad's horse. He stripped it of his saddle and looked it over.

"Least the little bastard could do is give you this saddle. I doubt anyone comes looking for it. There are no markings on it." Frank heaved it over the wagon's tailgate causing the bull and cow to stir a little.

Frank had picked up Toad's pistol off the ground from where it had fallen. He now inspected and unloaded it. He pocketed the bullets for himself. Hhe handed it to Levi and said, "If you're going to get into shooting scrapes you need to be better armed."

Frank tightened the cinch on his horse and took a length of rope to make a quick halter for Toad's horse. Before he climbed on his horse he chunked Toad's bridle into the wagon with the saddle.

The breakfast and the burial rejuvenated Frank. He had his old swagger back as he climbed on his horse. Lorelei handed Turon the sack of food supplies who in turn handed them to Frank.

"Much appreciated, ma'am," Frank said to Lorelei whose eyes still showed animosity. Looking down at the three, Frank said, "I won't tell you what name I'll use or what direction I intend to travel. I'll ride west from here but after that the less you know the less you can tell."

"I would travel by night close into settlements," Turon said.

Frank nodded and said nothing. He turned his horse west leading the late Toad Scraper's horse. The three watched as he crossed Chouteau Creek and rode west.

"Well, he was a better cowboy than he is an outlaw," Turon said watching him ride away.

"Did you see that bulge in his shirt?" asked Lorelei.

"He finally got his traveling money." Levi nodded.

Turon climbed into the wagon seat next to Lorelei

and let her drive the wagon. His shoulder, although he said it was better, was tender. Upon inspection by Lorelei, she saw it was swelling and starting to discolor.

Levi rode the bay. He had stuffed the revolver into the saddle bag. Turon loaned him five cartridges so he could leave the chamber under the hammer empty. Levi hoped he would not have use of it. Thinking of the events so far, he realized that all of it happened before most people had time to eat their breakfast.

CHAPTER 23

———◆»«◆»◆———

They traveled east. The land turned into a limestone prairie with rock outcrops running along the surface. Grass grew in abundance in the mineral rich ground. The rocks appearing like stone pavers on a city street.

They came across a set of railroad tracks running parallel by a well-worn wagon road. This was the Texas Road. A well-used route from Missouri to the south. A route that once connected the United States with Mexico and later the Republic of Texas. It was on this road they crossed Pryor Creek and continued north to a cut off road to the Markham Ferry.

Arriving in late afternoon the travelers waited for the ferry boat to cross back to their side. The Markham rates matched that of Stone's on the Verdigris. However, the Markham's did not discount for the colts and calf. This brought the crossing close to a dollar. Levi waited while the ferryman's son made change giving him back seven cents.

Like before, Turon and Lorelei crossed first in the wagon leading the cattle. This time Levi kept the strawberry roan mare snubbed close to the bay. The pinto tested the floor of the ferry boat like before. The roan stood still, however. The calf and colts again disembarked in theatrics.

Across the Grand they entered the Saline district of the Cherokee Nation. The land changed notably. This was where the southern plains met the Ozark Plateau. To the west lay open prairie all the way to the Rocky Mountains. To the east along the river cultivated fields laid around what was the town of Locust Grove. Beyond the town, hills lined the eastern horizon. Like sentinels these high ridges faced west and stood guard against the wild rolling prairies of the plains. White and red oak trees clung to the sides of the hills and needles of tall pines sang their songs in the breeze. Between the hills and ridges clear rushing streams flowed over gravel stream beds between giant sycamore trees to empty into the Grand River or what the Osage called Neosho.

They did not linger in Locust Grove. They needed no supplies, and the village did not offer much. They continued east, past a grove of ancient locust trees and a spring that rushed from beneath a limestone bluff. It was here during the Civil War that Union troops ambushed Confederate soldiers camped at the spring.

Thirty years earlier the same spot was the battle site between Cherokee and Osage fighting for use of the area. Countless other battles happened here. Some between men, some between man and beast. On this day, the late afternoon sun was warm and pleasant as Lorelei drove the wagon near the spring and stopped the team.

"We will not make the home place before dark. Might as well fill the water barrel and give the stock a drink." Turon directed Levi to the spring.

"A few weeks ago, we had to dig in the sand for water." Levi watched the spring water gush out from under a rock forming a stream.

"Wait till you taste this water. You do not have to

chew it." Turon smiled.

With the stock watered they traveled on. Lorelei talked to the mule and pinto urging them up a narrow wagon road. Giant oak trees and an occasional hickory blocked the sun as they climbed to the top of a ridge.

At the top, the trees thinned out and a rolling prairie opened to the east. They stayed on the wagon road. Several times riders stopped and hailed Turon. This was his country. Every mile brought them closer. Had he been alone and horseback he would have ridden into the night, but the mule and pinto were tired from the morning run.

"There is stand of persimmon trees about a half mile to the south. We can make camp there. Rest the stock. We will not make it tonight unless we tax these horses, and they are nearly played out," he said.

Lorelei gathered wood at the little persimmon grove while Turon and Levi tended the horses. Levi rubbed the bay down and combed her coat out. Out of oats and corn the pinto and mule grazed on the maturing grass.

"They will have corn tomorrow," Turon said.

"They deserve it, that pinto has earned his keep." Levi motioned to the horse grazing.

"I figure in a few days we can ride down to Tahlequah and see about a trading license." Turon watched the bull graze.

"Sounds good to me," Levi said. "How far away does Ounce live from your place?"

"Six miles maybe." Turon replied.

"Good. I need him to teach the roan some manners." Levi looked at the mustang mare.

"I am not sure I could have got that bull here without you, Little Kansas," Turon said.

"You would have managed." Levi assured him.

Lorelei called for supper, and they walked to the

wagon. This was the last supper they would share at the wagon. The last supper Lorelei would have to cook over an open fire. She was nervous to think what Turon's family would think of her. He had assured her that they would love and accept her as he had done. If they were half as kind as him then she had no real worries, she told herself.

The morning came with orange light breaking over the eastern horizon. While Lorelei made breakfast Turon sat cross-legged with a handful of persimmons and his folding pocketknife.

"What are you doing there?" Levi asked while pouring a cup of coffee.

"Splitting persimmons, Little Kansas." Turon said in an obvious tone.

"I see that, but why?" Levi asked seeking more clarification.

"Looking for spoons and forks." Turon studied the split halves of the persimmons.

"If you don't want to tell me then just say so." Levi took a drink of coffee.

"Look here, see the spoons?" Turon held a hand palm up for Levi to view.

"I see them," confirmed Levi.

"Well, spoons in the persimmons means there will be a wet snowy winter. Forks mean the winter will be dry and mild," Turon said as though instructing a child.

"You believe that?" Levi asked incredulously.

Lorelei chuckled and smiled. "You better believe it, Little Kansas."

"You got to know these things if you are going to live in the Nation. You do not want people thinking you are simple-minded."

"Okay, are they all spoons then?" Levi asked.

"Some are spoons, some are forks. More spoons than forks though." Turon studied the halves.

"What does that mean?"

"Means the winter will be cold and wet with some mild and dry times." Turon tossed the persimmons aside.

Levi rolled his eyes and Lorelei giggled as she removed the biscuits from the coals of the cook fire.

For the last time of the trip, they harnessed the mule and pinto. Turon tied the cow and bull to the wagon.

"Well, Bushyhead, you are almost home." Turon scratched bull's forelock.

They traveled east at a leisurely pace. Lorelei drove the team as Turon sat beside her pointing out landmarks and telling stories associated with them. They went by the Saline Courthouse, a tall white building standing among a small grove of trees. A spring gushed from a rock in front of the courthouse and people lounged in the shade. Waiting to do business in the courthouse, some waiting for a trial. Several knew Turon and came over and spoke in Cherokee with him. They eyed the bull with interest. They eyed Lorelei with more interest. Speaking Cherokee until they realized she did not speak it, then some switched to English.

Turon introduced Levi as Fighting Little Kansas, the man who captured Bill Kirby and beat him to the ground. A fair and honest man who planned to open a store but for now would be selling goods from his wagon. They eyed Levi in awe and all nodded and agreed there needed to be a store in the area.

"What all did you tell them?" Levi asked as they rode away from the district courthouse.

"I was just doing some advertising. They are excited about the store," Turon said.

"I do not have the money for a store yet," Levi said.

"Small details, Little Kansas." Turon laughed, his

spirit soaring the closer he got to home.

"East of here is a spring that runs into what becomes Spring Creek. People stop to water horses. Two trails cross there. It is halfway from Siloam Springs and Locust Grove. About halfway from the Delaware courthouse and Tahlequah. I think we should look at it. Be a good place to build a store or trade out of a wagon," Turon said.

"Sounds good to me." Levi nodded.

Leaving the Saline courthouse, they turned southeast and angled across the prairie until the land fell away to Spring Creek. As they dropped off the prairie once again, they were among giant oaks and hickory trees. They descended into the creek bottom on a wagon trace. The trace paralleled the creek. Sycamores blocked out the sun in places. Cane grew along the creek. Cattle grazed in fields of corn stubble. Other fields had grass cut for hay and stood short after greening up from September rains.

The excitement Turon felt was contagious. Lorelei and Levi, both felt it. Cows bawled across the creek and the bull answered in kind. He managed to pull loose from the wagon. He ran and bucked with his freedom toward the bawling cows.

Levi pitched the mare's lead lines to Turon.

"I'll bring him back." Levi started after the bull.

The bull crashed through a cane break and into the creek. Bawling his challenges to other bulls and announcing his arrival to the cows. Levi plunged the bay into the creek reaching down and grabbing the rope as it floated on the water.

Upstream in a deep pool of water a young woman stood in the creek. Her hands held long black hair lathered in soap suds. She stood bare, her clothes on the gravel bar next to the pool of water. She stared at Levi as he stared at her. She managed to turn her back to him and step deeper into the clear pool but continued to eye Levi over her shoulder.

The bull paid no attention to the young woman in the water and started to climb out of the creek bed toward the cows. The spell of the young bare-backed Cherokee woman that had transfixed Levi broke when the bull's lead rope started to leave his grip. He quickly recovered and took several turns around the saddle horn. He turned the bull. Levi and the bay dragged him back across the creek through the cane break. The bull obeyed the rope showing only a little protest.

Leaving the young woman washing her hair in the creek Levi caught up with the wagon.

"I tried to tell you to let him go if you could not catch him. He is home," Turon said.

Soon they approached a well-established farm. The house, barn, and several outbuildings sat reflecting fifty years of improvements. Fruit trees lined a well-maintained rail fence.

Several hounds came out from under the porch of a square log house built against the south facing hillside. They barked and bayed until Turon's sharp command silenced them. A Cherokee woman in her late forties stood on the porch. From a barn stepped a Cherokee man in his upper forties and a boy the mirror image of what Turon must have looked like ten years earlier.

Upon seeing Turon they all rushed to the wagon. Turon climbed down to embrace his mother, father and his brother rushed in as well. In Cherokee Turon introduced Lorelei. His mother's eyes widened and in rapid Cherokee she berated Turon for not writing. She hit Turon in the right shoulder with an open hand slap causing him to wince in pain. Then they welcomed Lorelei into their family. Once Lorelei was on the ground Turon's mother embraced the nervous young woman in a hug.

Levi sat on the bay until Turon urged him down. Turning to his family Turon spoke in Cherokee at length. His mother eyed Levi and his father nodded. They approached Levi and in English made him feel welcomed. His father looked the bull over approving the purchase making remarks in Cherokee then repeating them for Levi's ears in English.

Turon had one arm around Lorelei recounting the highlights of the trip. Levi saw something or someone catch Turon's eyes causing him to smile big and speak in Cherokee once again. Levi turned to see the young woman who had been in the creek. She stood close and shook Levi's hand as Turon introduced them. Levi could smell the lavender soap she had used, and her wet hair pulled back into a ponytail.

Levi stood mesmerized and matched the stare from Turon's sister.

"Little Kansas, this is my sister Ruth. Ruth, meet Little Kansas."

In a moment of great clarity. Levi knew he would never leave the Cherokee Nation.

Afterword

Although the characters in this book are fictional except for a few historical cameo appearances the land is real. Where Turon and Levi "Little Kansas" travel and camp are places you can visit today. If you are in Oklahoma many of the locations would make a good weekend trip.

Thanks to the rocky terrain and controlled burns the Tall Grass Prairie is still intact in Osage County, Oklahoma. Washington Irving made a month-long journey in 1832 with an army patrol through what is now Oklahoma. He wrote in his journal that they were never out of sight of smoke from a grassfire.

The Osage and tribes before them set the prairie on fire to promote new growth of grasses. The new tender grass attracted buffalo, elk, and many other animals. Berries would grow in abundance in the burned over areas. Invasive tree sprouts would burn and burst in the heat as these fires burned. Ensuring it stayed a sea of grass.

Accessed by county roads north of Pawhuska, Oklahoma the Nature Conservancy has collected some thirty thousand acres of the prairie. You can drive through it today and see buffalo graze as they did ten thousand years ago. As a child of the Ozark Plateau and spending much of my life in Oklahoma, Kansas and Texas I refer to bison as buffalo. I know it is not the modern nomenclature to use. To correct me in emails or on social media would be a waste of time.

One hundred miles to the west is the National Salt Plains Wildlife Refuge and Salt Plains State Park. A large deposit of salt provides migratory birds with nesting grounds in the fall and winter. Summertime is wide open for people who want to dig for salt crystals. The state park offers cabins and camping sites.

Where Turon and Levi meet the mounted patrol is now the Little Sahara State Park. Sand dunes offer those with dune buggies and side by sides a chance to off road. Also, near by although it did not make the book is the Alabaster Caverns State Park where you can go into a cave and see bats cling to the rock ceiling.

The canyon where Turon meets Lorelei is now Roman Nose State Park. The spring still runs strong and there are hiking trails you can take. You can play golf where they left Lorelei's dead mule for the buzzards. Horseback riding is available upon reservations. Canoeing, kayaking, and swimming are all allowed. Like in the book, time has a way of slipping by in the canyon.

Tulsey Town or now Tulsa, Oklahoma is no longer a cowtown. Although the Tulsa Stockyards still does a good deal of business on Mondays. The Original house of the Reverend Morris still stands near the intersection of Edison Street and Country Club Drive. It is the oldest structure in Tulsa and stands as it did in the book.

Bridges have replaced the ferries across the Verdigris and Grand Rivers. The Mayes County Historical Society and Museum in Pryor Creek, Oklahoma has some great pictures, maps, and items to view on the area. Bass fishermen and water sports have replaced the fertile farmland with Lake Hudson. East of Locust Grove on Scenic 412 highway a roadside park sets where Turon and Levi fill the water barrel on their wagon.

Further east and just south of Scenic 412 the Saline Courthouse of the Cherokee Nation still stands. This was the legal center of the area during the nineteenth century. Prior to that other tribes and those who came before held council and camped at the spring on the property.

Before the Cherokee Nation remodeled and reopened it as a museum it was a place to take your girlfriend. Ghosts protected the area and the virtue of young women. As owls and other night animals would send young people running back to cars and pickups.

As a father of two daughters and now that I live back in the area. I prefer the museum and well-kept grounds over the abandoned haunt it once was.

Every corner of the State of Oklahoma offers unique history. The history did not begin with the land run or in 1907 at statehood. Hunters and gatherers who we know nothing about hunted mastodons. They laughed, cried, and lived as only they knew how.

The Caddo and Wichitas built homes. The Spanish came and sought gold. Comanches came later and found buffalo in golden sunsets. Frenchmen trapped and traded for furs. Eastern tribes finally found a place to rest only to be torn apart by civil war.

Our ancestors were legends. In the book you just finished and the series to follow, I intend to introduce you to those legends. Thank you for reading, remember to rate and review. Be good and make good choices.

ABOUT THE AUTHOR

Born and raised on the Ozark Plateau. Charlie Amos grew up in the footsteps of outlaws, cowboys, and woodsmen. He currently lives in Oklahoma with his wife, children, and dog Banjo. When he is not tending cattle and kids he is reading and writing about the American West. Years of working in agriculture, forestry, trucking, and teaching school has laid the foundation of telling our American story through relatable characters. Writing westerns for westerners, and everyone else.

www.ingramcontent.com/pod-product-compliance
Lightning Source LLC
Chambersburg PA
CBHW061216170626
46809CB00003B/1374